THE COAT

EVELYN ALLEN HARPER

Ink Smith Publishing

www.ink-smith.com

The final approval for this literary material is granted by the author. All characters appearing in this work are fictitious. Any resemblance to real persons, living or dead, is purely coincidental.

Cover Image created by: Rowenna Anderson

ISBN: 978-1-939156-22-8

Ink Smith Publishing

P.O Box 1086

Glendora CA

****

Other Books By Evelyn Allen Harper

The Accidental Mystery Series

And So To Sleep

And So To Dream

The Wrath of Grapes

And So To Love

And So It Goes

The Wrath of Winter

The Coat

CHAPTER 1

It was happening again.

Waves of terror left him breathless. He waited in the black silence of his bedroom, his senses on high alert. The squeaking of the loose stair railing could have been part of a dream, albeit a reoccurring dream. But what if it wasn't a dream this time?

In one fluid movement, he jerked the sheets over the lined up pillows and rolled under the bed. Don't move don't even think close your eyes hold your breath is this the end?

His mind raced as he waited to be found. For ten years, plastic surgery and hiding had kept him alive. But his reclusive life was dull and living under the threat of death was exhausting. Maybe it was time to accept the inevitable and….

The familiar voice that whispered his name changed everything. Any fear that he had been feeling turned into instant rage. It still might be his end, but not without a fight.

What he hadn't expected to see peering into his hiding place was the face that belonged to the familiar voice.

"No!" he screamed.

The Coat

Jerked from his nightmare, he sat up. The hands that he ran over his face were shaking and his heart was threatening to jump out of his chest.

The face.

He knew it well.

CHAPTER 2

"Bye, Mom!"

Gritting her teeth, Julia put the car into reverse and peered into her rearview mirror. She could do this! The lone little sapling that her mother kept replacing at the end of the long driveway seemed a mile away. Holding her breath, she slowly eased the car backwards, determined that this time she would make it. The little tree was looming large in her rearview mirror when a rap on her window, a lapse of concentration, and a jerk of the wheel shattered her good intentions.

"Muh...thur!"

"Oh, I'm so sorry, honey!"

"I really thought I was going to make it this time," Julie wailed. "What's wrong?"

Her mother pushed a plastic bag through the open window. "You forgot the left-overs."

The wonderful smell of Thanksgiving dinner oozing out of the bag was enough to melt Julia's agitation. "Oh, thanks, Mom! Now move away."

"Watch out for the sapling!" her mother called.

Julia continued her backward journey, stopping only long enough to wave goodbye to her mother. As she straightened the car, the sudden feeling of liberation that swept through her quickly disappeared at the sight of her mother wiping her eyes. How could she feel so joyful about returning to her independent life when it made her mother so sad?

As Julia drove along northern Michigan's popular Route 22, she wasn't admiring the scenery; she was reveling in the joy of driving her new car. Smiling, she reached out a hand and swept it over the shining dashboard. Her trip home for the Thanksgiving holiday had held more promise than just a turkey dinner; her mother had bought her a car. The little red sports car had been parked in the driveway when she arrived home. It was her first year of teaching, and combined with the expense of renting a small apartment and making payments on her student loan, saving for a car had been out of the question. Even though it wasn't a brand new car, it still had the smell and look of one. Now because she had her own wheels, she wouldn't have to wait in the wind, rain, and snow at the bus stop. Julia cringed at the thought that she wasn't so independent after all; she still needed her mother to buy her a car. She pushed the troubling thought aside and tightened her grip on the steering wheel.

The Sunday traffic was light. There were whole stretches where she and her convertible had the road all to themselves. Life was good! It would have been even better with the top down, but it was a bit too chilly for that.

The Thanksgiving break that she had looked forward to had come and gone. There would be no more days away from the classroom until Christmas. Twenty-two more days until she would again be making the drive home for her mother's stuffing. Julia shifted in her seat when reality hit; fifteen of those days were class days, starting tomorrow. Her foot eased up on the gas pedal and the smile on her face vanished. She hadn't made lesson plans for the coming week. Her intentions had been good, but with the excitement of the new car, she had never gotten around to it. Tomorrow, when her classroom door opened, thirty eighth-grade bodies exploding with hormones would rush into the room eager to assault her for the rest of the day. It made her tired just thinking about what was involved in writing the plans. Would it be so terrible if she didn't do any planning for tomorrow? It would just be for one day. How bad could that be? After promising herself that she'd make the rest of the week's plans on Monday evening, she pulled into McDonald's drive-through. A cup of coffee would be her reward for making such a good decision.

A voice came over the sound system asking for her order.

"A small black coffee, please," she yelled into the speaker.

"You want fries with that?" a bored voice asked.

"No, thank you!"

After paying for her coffee at the first window, she drove to the second window where an employee, holding her coffee in his hand, leaned out and intently studied her car. Julia extended her hand to take her coffee but the server seemed to have forgotten she was there. Julia watched his eyes pass over the car from bumper to bumper twice before she cleared her throat.

"Uh, my coffee please?" she asked gesturing to the cup in his hand.

"What? Oh, sorry about that!" With a flash of white teeth and a twinkle in his merry brown eyes, he handed her the coffee.

Julia nodded her thanks and drove away.

* * * *

Apples don't fall very far from the tree, mused Susan as she watched her daughter's continued struggle to back the car out of the long driveway. If the inability to master the art of driving backwards was a genetic disorder, then she had passed that to Julia along with the blonde hair and blue eyes.

She held her breath until her daughter made it to the road; the little oak, the third attempt at foliage near the end of her driveway, was still standing.

Susan had a lump in her throat as her only child drove away. The house was always so quiet after Julia left; it took days for her to feel comfortable in it again. Her friend, Emma, from her office was always telling her to get a cat.

"You'd never be alone then," Emma would say. Brushing a solitary tear from her cheek, Susan, a residential real estate agent, headed to the den to organize her schedule for tomorrow. Keeping her mind busy with work details helped her adjust to her once again empty house. She flipped open the folder that contained the information on a house Allen Real Estate had just listed. Her transferee had left her a message that he would be back in town, and asked if she could she show him more houses. Since he had already seen the houses in his price range, the new listing was all that that she had to show him.

Monday morning dawned bright and noisy. Raucous birds outside the bedroom window woke Susan and the slant of sun stabbing into her eyes kept her awake. Groaning, her first impulse to pull the pillow over her head and go back to sleep was shoved aside when she remembered today's appointment with the handsome Charles Holiday. Transferring into the northern Michigan region from Pittsburgh, he had met her on his first trip to the area. He had visited several more times, and each time he'd requested that she show him houses. Today she and Charles would meet at the new listing at two o'clock.

Susan didn't allow herself to figure out why she was spending more time than usual on her appearance this morning. After three outfit changes, she finally settled on the long-sleeved red dress she had bought on impulse last week. Standing in front of the mirror viewing her reflection, the thought that maybe the dress was a bit too short was quickly dismissed. She reasoned that the dress only looked so short because her legs were long and she was wearing heels. After a close inspection of her freshly shampooed blonde hair and her artfully made up face, once again her eyes swept down to her shoes. She frowned, and reluctantly stepped out of them. Granted, the high-heeled shoes went well with the dress, but with them on she looked like someone who was dressing for a date. For heaven's sake, she was only showing the man a house. Susan didn't allow herself to wonder why she was looking forward to seeing her Pittsburgh buyer. After selecting a shoe with a much lower heel, she grabbed her purse and her car keys.

While backing her car down the long driveway, she grinned, remembering her daughter's recent struggle to stay on the driveway. The grin evaporated when, with a bump, her car backed over the little sapling.

Apples don't fall very far from the tree.

CHAPTER 3

Charles Holiday yawned as he marked the page in the book he was reading before placing it on the coffee table. Engrossed in the plot, he had almost convinced himself that last night's nightmare hadn't happened. It wasn't that he was unfamiliar with the bad dream. Unfortunately, over the past ten years he had been awakened by the same one many times. But last night's nightmare was frightfully different; the voice now had a face. It was a face he knew far too well.

All through breakfast and lunch, the lingering feeling from last night's dream hung over him like a black cloud. Unable to shake it off, he was in the bathroom splashing cold water on his face when a chance glance at the clock reminded him that he had an appointment. Time had gotten away from him; he was going to be late.

The trick of staying active while retaining a low profile was a continuous problem. His latest venture to get himself showered, dressed, and out of the house was playing the single man looking to purchase a home. How much trouble could he get into just by meeting a realtor to see a house? Grinning, he thought about today's attractive realtor; getting into trouble with her could be interesting. Shaking his head, he tried not to think about the time in his life when he would have hotly pursued the idea.

He thought about the information he had given Susan, a realtor, whose last name he couldn't remember. He did not live in Pittsburgh, he had no intention of buying a house, and his name wasn't Charles Holiday. When she asked about his marital status, he'd told her he wasn't married.

A careful study of his face in the mirror before leaving his apartment assured him that he had done all he could to alter his appearance. He couldn't do anything about his height and body build, but plastic surgery had modified his features and a change of hair color from brown to blonde had added to the deception. He'd tried growing hair on his face, but since the whiskers appeared in a different color than his dyed hair, it hadn't worked. Even with all the changes, he was constantly fearful that the people who were looking for him wouldn't be fooled.

Susan, whose last name he still couldn't remember, was certainly someone he'd like to get to know better…but just as a friend. *No*, he told himself, he couldn't even think about her like that. There was no place in his life for that kind of relationship, or any kind of relationship. Knowing that realtors work on commission did make him feel a bit guilty about taking up her time. Maybe he would ask her out for coffee after they saw the house. *No,* he told himself again, *stop thinking that way. it wouldn't be fair to her.*

* * * *

The vacant house Susan had scheduled to show Charles was listed by Allen Real Estate. Vacant houses usually have a key inside a lockbox that's attached to the doorknob, and the realtor who wants to show the house is given the combination to open it. But the owners of the house had made it a condition of the listing that there would be no easy access. The listing office had been issued one key with strict orders from the seller not to have duplicates made. For an agent, it's a pain to have to pick up a key before a showing and another pain having to return it. It was both time consuming and time constricting. There always seemed to be another realtor waiting for the key to be returned.

Upon opening the door to the office, Susan's nose was assaulted by the smell of a wet dog. She paused in the doorway looking for the source of the odor. In one corner of the room, slumped on a ragged, blue and white checkered mattress, was a dog so large his barrel shaped chest hung over the sides.

The person at the front desk looked up and grinned at her.

"Sorry about the smell," she said. "Lucky had a bath this morning."

Susan recognized the dog from his pictures in the paper. The massive mutt made the front page more times than the mayor. Sometimes the story that accompanied the picture was pretty far-fetched, at least in Susan's opinion. The most recent claim was that Lucky had saved a cat from a fire. He had accompanied the fire truck to the house and risked a fiery death to save the gray, grumpy-looking cat named Happy.

The woman at the desk stood up. "I don't believe we've met. I'm Clara Skinner, and are you Susan Cook?"

Clara Skinner's picture had been in the paper almost as much as her dog's. Susan couldn't remember how many times this Clara woman had been named Realtor of the Year.

Handing one of her business cards to Clara, Susan smiled. "That's me."

"Well, I probably don't need to tell you, but since my client is pretty picky, before you leave make sure you've turned off all the lights, and please check that the door is securely locked when you leave."

Susan nodded. "I've had picky sellers, too."

"Oh, one more thing," Clara said while handing her the key. "There's another showing later today, so would you please bring the key back as soon as you're finished with it?"

"Of course, I will," Susan said her eyes glued to the massive dog. "How do you give a dog that big a bath?" she asked suddenly.

Clara chuckled. "I'm married to the fire chief here in town. The guys just turn the hose they use to clean their equipment on him, lather him up, and then rinse him off. If I didn't have the firemen's help, I might have to send him through the car wash!"

Susan was laughing as she left the office.

CHAPTER 4

Susan was sitting in the driveway of the vacant house when her customer, in a rusty dull red car, drove up beside her. Surprised at the shabby appearance of the car, an unsettling thought hit her: how qualified a buyer was this man? Since she had always driven both of them to the appointments, she was seeing his car for the first time. The houses she had been showing him were highly priced. If he could only afford a beat-up junker to drive, then how was he going to afford the house? Puzzled, Susan watched Charles unwind his tall body from the constraint of his small car. Thoughts of qualification fled Susan's mind when, in greeting, he opened her car door and held out his hand. With one tug on her short skirt, she smiled up at him, grasped his hand, and let him help her out of the car. Susan felt the warmth of a blush when he held her hand a bit longer than necessary. Flustered, she released his hand to rummage through her purse searching for the key to the house.

"Found it!" she smiled up at him. "Ready?"

"Lead the way," Charles said grinning down at her. She swallowed hard and led him up to the front door.

Unlocking the door was becoming a problem. He was standing so close behind her she could feel the heat radiating from his body. The response to his nearness was also disturbing. Without a conscious thought, she leaned back until her body made contact with Charles. She was so shocked at what she had done that her fingers turned to thumbs; she dropped the key.

"Oops!" she muttered as she bent down to pick it up...and so did Charles. When their heads hit together with a resounding whack, Susan stepped back, lost her balance, and landed on her backside.

"Oh, I'm so sorry! Are you hurt?" Charles asked as he held out his hand.

Susan pulled at her short skirt and hoped her face wasn't too red. Grabbing his hand, she allowed him to pull her to her feet.

"No, I'm not hurt, I'm...." Susan paused when she saw that Charles was trying to keep a straight face. "You're going to laugh, aren't you?"

Wiping the grin off his face was difficult. "I'm sorry, but you have to admit...."

Susan dismissed his apology with a toss of her head. "I'm glad you're so easily amused. Now where's the key?"

Charles handed it to her. "I'm so sorry I laughed. But it *was* funny!"

Susan gave him a dirty look.

"Okay, I apologize again. Could I, uh, could you, uh, oh hell! Would you have coffee with me after we see the house? My head hurts, and I'll bet yours does too. We both need a caffeine hit."

Susan hesitated. He had said that he wasn't married. But even if he were, what harm would a cup of coffee do to his marriage?

She rubbed her head. "I think I'll take you up on the offer."

As the two roamed through the house, Charles remembered to act interested, asking enough questions to establish himself as a potential buyer.

"When was the house built?" he asked staring at a particularly interesting bit of decoration around the doorframe. The hideous little cherub was aiming arrows down the hall.

"About twelve years ago," Susan responded. Tilting her head, she looked into his eyes and laughed. "Don't worry. The arrow isn't pointed at you."

Whoa! For a brief moment, their eyes locked. Charles blinked. The space between them felt charged with electricity.

Susan caught her breath, quickly looked away, and changed the subject. "And here we have the kitchen," she babbled. "Don't you just love all that granite?"

After locking the house, Susan drove to the real estate office to return the key. Clara and the big dog weren't there, but the smell still was. The person who took the key, a petite green-eyed redhead, was holding a phone to her ear.

"Well, as much as I feel for the woman, she shouldn't have dropped our firm," she said before noticing Susan. She smiled, took the key from Susan, and kept talking.

"Eighty thousand dollars!" Susan heard her exclaim as she headed for the door. "Well," the voice continued, "that's what people get when they don't work with professionals!"

* * * *

When Susan walked into the Omelet Shop, Charles was already seated at a table. Ever since her husband's untimely death she'd asked the same question: why are all the interesting men already married? But here she was, about to have coffee with a very handsome, interesting, and according to him, unmarried man.

By the time she arrived at the table he was standing, holding her chair. The conversation over coffee was comfortable. She couldn't remember the last time she'd had such a relaxed chat with a man. They laughed over their mutually bumped heads, and when it was time to leave, he walked her to her car while assuring her that he would contact her again the next time he was in town.

CHAPTER 5

Julia sat at her desk, her head in her hands as the class of eighth graders filed noisily out of the room. The last hour had been hell; in fact, the whole day had been a disaster. She took a deep breath, held it, and then felt her body shudder as she released it. To be honest with herself, she had to accept part of the blame for the chaos that had brought the principal to her room demanding to know why she had lost control of her class.

Julia had hung her head, apologized, and promised it wouldn't happen again. How could she explain to Mrs. Sheldon that she had spent her lesson-planning time driving around in her new car? She had just had her first glimpse of what thirteen-year-old eighth graders can do to a teacher when they sense a weakness.

Still holding her head, a deep voice made her drop her hands and look up.

"Wh…what did you say?" she stammered.

"Was it really that bad?"

Julia found herself staring into the biggest, kindest brown eyes she had ever seen. One thing that always made her tear-up was someone offering her sympathy.

"Oh, I'm sorry," she sniffed. "But, yes, it really was that bad."

Taking advantage of the box of tissues on her desk, he pulled one out and handed it to her. "And I thought I was having a rough time. Eighth graders really know how to humble a substitute teacher! I think my class was as unruly as yours. I could hear you yelling the whole way down to my room."

Julia stopped wiping her eyes. "Was I really that loud?"

"Afraid so," he chuckled. "By the way, I'm Denny McCain."

Julia stood up. "I must look a mess," she apologized.

Grinning, he pointed a finger at her face. "Just a little bit of mascara here and there."

Julia scrubbed her face with the tissue. "I'm Julia Cook, first year teacher...and it shows, I'm afraid."

"Well, I'm glad to meet you, Julia. We'll be running into each other again, I'm sure. I'm replacing Mrs. Weber who's taking maternity leave."

Julia was counting. "Three weeks before the baby is due, plus six weeks after. I count about nine weeks?"

"At least. I had given up hope of getting a teaching job anywhere. No nearby school district has been hiring new teachers this year, so with my college diploma in one hand and a spatula in the other, I've been flipping burgers at McDonald's ever since graduation."

Julia tilted her head and looked at him. There was something about his eyes that looked familiar. "Well, I guess congratulations are in order then!"

"Thank you! By the way, do you know who owns that spiffy red convertible in the parking lot? I think I saw one like it yesterday."

Julia beamed. "That spiffy red convertible is mine!"

Denny hit his forehead with the back of his hand. "You! It was you!"

"Me?" Julia looked around. "What did I do?"

"I saw you at McDonald's yesterday."

Of course those eyes looked familiar. "Oh, yes! I remember you now! I also remember that I had to remind you to hand me my coffee."

"I was lusting after your car," Denny laughed. "Take me for a ride in it someday?"

Julia grinned. "I just might do that!"

Denny turned to leave. "It was nice meeting you, Julia. See you around!"

She watched the tall, broad-shouldered substitute teacher walk away. Maybe her mother had had ulterior motives when she bought the red convertible for her single daughter.

* * * *

Denny McCain walked by the red convertible on the way to his car. *What a sweet ride* he thought. Maybe, *if* Mrs. Weber changes her mind and wants to stay home with her baby, and *if* they offer me the job to finish the school year, and *if* I can get caught up on some of my past debts, and *if* I can afford to move out of my dad's house, and *if*....

Denny shook his head. There were too many ifs between him and a replacement of the rusted junker of a car he presently owned. At least it started most of the time.

A half hour later he was still sitting in his car, unable to get the stubborn engine to turn over when he saw the convertible's owner walk into the parking lot. His pride was begging that she wouldn't notice him in his crappy car.

"Hey, Denny, having car trouble?"

Damn! "Looks like it," he called back.

"Can I help?"

Denny felt his face redden. Oh well, she would probably find out eventually that he still lived with his dad. Might as well get it over with.

"I really don't want to call a tow truck," he yelled back. "My dad's a whiz with cars, but unfortunately, his car is at the dealers today getting detailed. Could you drive to my house and get my dad? He usually can get my car started." Denny, his face red, barely made eye contact with Julia. He buried his hands in his pockets and looked down at his shoes.

Twenty-four-year-old guys are supposed to be living on their own and have cars that start if they want the pretty girl to notice them, Denny thought sourly.

"I guess you're going to get a ride in my spiffy red convertible sooner than either one of us thought," Julia laughed. "Come on, get in." Julia watched Denny lock his car door manually and climb into the passenger seat.

"Is this leather?" he asked touching the seat. Julia grinned at him,

"Sure is."

Denny clicked the seatbelt and slouched back. Julia could feel the embarrassment radiating off of him. She reached out and lightly touched his shoulder.

"Before this, I took the bus," she confided, "I would have given anything to even have a car that didn't start, especially on the days it rained."

Denny smiled feebly, and pulled his phone out of his pocket. Fumbling with the buttons and feeling like a complete loser, he left a message for his father.

Twenty minutes later Julia pulled to the curb in front of a beautiful little Cape Cod that had ivy crawling up the sides. Stepping off the porch and walking toward them was a man who looked so much like Denny that Julia thought it must be Denny's older brother.

"Julia, meet my dad, Dennis McCain, Senior. Dad, this is Julia Cook, she's an eighth-grade teacher at my school."

I'm seeing double, Julie thought. Both were tall and broad shouldered, and both had a head of thick brown hair that was identically cut. The only difference she could see was in the eyes. Denny, the son, had laughing brown eyes; the father's brown eyes had a hard look about them.

Dennis Senior grunted as he squeezed into the back seat. "Glad to meet you, Miss Cook. So, dumbhead, where's the car this time?"

"Back in the school's parking lot."

"That's twenty minutes away, isn't it? I have no intention of walking back home if we can't get it started, so Miss Cook, could you stick around until we figure out what's wrong with it this time?"

Julia had a troubled look on her face. Denny's dad called him a dumbhead? Then she noticed they were looking at her, waiting for an answer.

"Of course I will! This time, huh? I take it this has happened before?"

Dennis Senior rolled his eyes and grumbled.

****

With both of their heads shoved under the hood of the car, all Julia could see of the two men was their identical backsides. She waited in her car until Denny pulled his head out, crawled into his car, and attempted to start it. After a few sick coughs, the engine caught. Dennis Senior slammed the hood closed, then turned toward Julia and waved. Julia waved back, put her car in gear, and drove out of the parking lot.

Denny watched the red convertible disappear into the lane of traffic. Could anything be more humiliating than admitting to a beautiful girl that you still lived at home? It would have been even worse if she had gotten out of her car. Then she would have heard his dad cursing Denny's profession, his rattletrap of a car, his inability to fix anything, and his life in general. Denny closed his eyes and thanked God she'd stayed in the car.

Denny had sat behind the wheel in the school parking lot watching his dad's frowning face staring at him through the windshield. His dad's lips had been moving. Denny wasn't very good at lip reading, but since he had heard the same words coming out of his dad's mouth since childhood, he was quite aware of what his dad was yelling at him. Embedded somewhere in the string of cuss words would be three important words: start…the… car.

Denny had closed his eyes, turned the key, and prayed that the motor would catch. When it did, he forced a smile as his dad crawled back into the car. When Denny thanked his father for coming to the rescue, Dennis had looked at him hard, rolled his eyes, and grunted.

CHAPTER 6

Charles stared at his front door. The black thread he'd caught in the latch wasn't there; someone had opened the door while he was gone. The feeling that eyes were watching him put speed into his sprint to the car. With squealing tires, he whipped his car around and sped away from his house seconds before he heard the sound of gunshots.

Since he hadn't seen a strange car near his house he figured he had a head start, but just in case, he turned and twisted for miles. In the ten years he'd been hiding from them, they'd found him several times. He had established the habit of circling his current residence a few times before he actually pulled into the driveway.

He shuddered when he remembered the first time when, new at the game, he hadn't thought ahead about what he would do if they found him. That missing element almost got him killed. It had been a dangerous way to learn that good escape plans were essential if he wanted to stay alive.

Just as soon as he felt sure he wasn't being followed, he'd switch the car for one of several he had stashed around town to take him to the next step in his escape.

Taking a shaky breath, he congratulate himself for once again evading those who were being paid to kill him. Of all the places he had fled to for safety, he'd liked living in the little town in northern Michigan the best; he hated to leave. It saddened him to realize he didn't have the luxury of choosing where he lived. Why hadn't he kept his mouth shut ten years ago? But he hadn't, and what was done was done.

Deep in thought, he missed the first time the engine sputtered but not the second. Was something wrong? In answer to his question, the engine gave one last cough and died. Charles pressed on the gas but the car only rolled a few more feet and refused to continue. Glancing down at the dashboard, Charles noted the gas tank was reading empty. One of the bullets must have nicked the gas tank. Charles counted himself lucky that his pursuers hadn't invested in explosive bullets.

Looking around, Charles didn't see anyone but if it meant anything, the hair on the back of his neck was standing up. To top it off, he had no idea where he was. His knuckles whitened as he clutched the steering wheel in frustration.

He had driven a circuitous route full of twists and turns for miles to make sure no one was following him. The chance that his car had become disabled within walking distance of one of his hidden ones was slim.

The closest street light was a few blocks away. Charles pulled out his emergency map but it was too dark for him to read. He tucked it into his jacket, turned the car off, and stuffed the keys into his pocket.

Charles walked to the nearest intersection and read the street signs. He groaned when he figured that the closest hidden car was at least ten miles away. The gang chasing him would eventually find his abandoned car, and knowing he was on foot, they would track him down.

Susan.

Now why had her name popped into his head? He didn't know where she lived and he didn't want to get her involved in his mess. But what if he didn't involve her, just take her car? He needed wheels to get to the next step in his escape. If not Susan, then who? Come to think of it, he didn't even know her last name, but she'd given him one of her business cards. He released the breath he was holding when her card turned up in one of his pockets. Ah, her last name was Cook. Charles turned back to the car.

A quick search for the phone book that was under the same seat as the map, another trip made to the streetlight to find her address, and then, with the map, he found her street. It was within walking distance.

Leaving his car where it had died, he started out on foot. Finding street names and matching them with his map soon had him in her neighborhood. After finding the street, he circled her house several times. Dare he get her mixed up in his problems? Looking through the window at the inviting, lighted house, he tried to talk himself out of involving her. She would be in danger just by associating with him. Where else could he go? He knew how the gang worked. They'd be watching every motel and hotel in the small town just waiting for him to show up.

Charles stared at the house from across the street. Susan's house was brightly lit inside. Charles could picture her sitting on the couch with a cup of tea and a romance novel. She seemed like the type who would indulge in a risqué novel once in awhile. His body reacted when he imagined what it would be like to curl up on the couch with her. She was attracted to him…he could tell. Remembering how flustered she'd been when he pulled her to her feet this afternoon made him smile.

A bedroom light went on in Susan's house jarring him back to reality. He crossed the street and paused at the end of her driveway. They couldn't possibly think she had anything to do with this if he just stole her car. No, on second thought, that was a bad idea. It wouldn't be fair to involved Susan in any way. Hotwiring a stolen car was a better idea. His decision made, he turned to walk away when men on foot appeared out of nowhere. They were coming up the street the same way Charles had.

Silently he prayed as he ran, "Forgive me, Susan, for what I'm about to get you into."

CHAPTER 7

Julia chuckled to herself as she drove. Her mom was always asking if anything interesting had happened during her day, and this was sort of interesting, it was at least worth a call home. Her mom had looked so sad yesterday evening when she left that she was glad for a reason to check in with her. Darkness was coming fast at the end of an over-cast day, and a glance at her iPhone made her realize that she'd spent more time with the McCain duo than she'd thought. A voice command to her phone connected her to her mom's cell. When her mom didn't answer after ten rings, Julia ended the call and speed-dialed the real estate office.

"Hello, Town and Country Real Estate, how may I help you?" asked a friendly voice.

"Oh, hi, Emma! I'm glad you're still there. Oh, by the way, it's Julia. I'm looking for my mother. Is she there?"

"Hi Julia! I haven't had a chance to talk to you in a long time. How's the teaching job going?"

Julia snorted. "Emma, don't ask a question like that if you aren't ready to hear the answer."

"All is not peaches and cream, I take it?"

"Today it was more like rotten peaches and soured cream."

"That bad, eh?"

"Yes, that bad. I even got into trouble with the principal."

Emma snickered.

"I heard that, Emma! And it wasn't funny, believe me. But I called to talk to mom. Is she there?"

"No, your mom isn't here. The last time I saw her she was heading out to meet her Pittsburgh buyer. I know she showed him a house and returned the key to Allen Real Estate after the showing. I was talking to Molly Hatch, the owner, when your mom returned it."

"Well, she's not at home. She probably stopped at the grocery store. I'll wait a bit and try again. Thanks Emma."

"Hey Julia, I meant it. I miss the nice chats you and I used to have before you got all grown-up. I'm here if you really want to unload your troubles on someone. I get tired rehashing my own."

"I just might take you up on that one day. Bye!"

Julia pulled into her driveway and laid her head back on the headrest and closed her eyes. It had been a long day. Taking her lesson planning material from the backseat, she started for her apartment door but the darkening of the sky caught her attention. She dropped her things off at her door and went back to cover her shiny new car.

With the task completed, Julia, went inside, and after heating up some Thanksgiving leftovers, she booted up her computer. She had promised herself that she would work on lesson plans, but she couldn't help opening up her web browser and scrolling through the latest status updates of her friends.

Her messenger went off with a bloop! and her mother's name popped up on her screen.

Susan: How was work?

Julia: Awful, the class was really loud today. One of the teachers, almost on the other side of the building, heard me shouting, and even the Principal came to have a word with me.

Susan: ☹ Did you get to your lesson plans?

Julia: No, I'm going to start them soon though. I had to help another teacher get his car started so I was late getting home.

Susan: His?

Julia: Mom.

Susan: Is he cute?

Julia: Stop it.

Susan: I bet he's one of those sensitive types with big soulful eyes.

Julia: Nice try, Mom. I'm going to change into something comfortable and start working on my lesson plans.

Susan: I probably should change, too. I'm still in my work clothes.

Julia: LOL Your *work* clothes?

Susan: Hey, don't scoff! Showing houses is work!

Julia: Sure it is, Mom. What did you wear today?

Susan: Something you've never seen. I bought it last week.

Julia: Would I like to borrow it?

Susan: Hmmm. Am I going to have to put a lock on my closet door?

Julia: As long as we stay the same size, yes.

Susan: Oh, someone just rang the doorbell…I can see out the window. It's my Pittsburgh buyer! What in the world is he doing here? Now you get off the computer and stop procrastinating!

Julia: Were you expecting him?

Julia: Mom?

Julia: Everything OK?

When her mother didn't answer her, Julia started to worry. Why would a buyer be visiting her mother this late in the day?

Shrugging, Julia hoped her mom was enjoying his visit. Focusing on her lesson plan for tomorrow Julia closed her laptop and poured over *Flowers for Algernon* looking for something that would inspire her to get her class focused and interested in what she had to say.

CHAPTER 8

Susan hadn't heard a car pull into her driveway, but by peeking out a side window she could see that indeed it was her Pittsburgh buyer at her front door. The surprise turned into something else when, after opening it, Charles slid in and closed the door.

Breathing hard, he gasped, "Turn off the lights!"

Susan froze. Stories of real estate crimes flashed through her head. Just recently, a couple had returned to their house after a showing and found the dead agent stuffed into a closet. And then there was the agent who was raped....

Charles had found and flipped the switch, plunging the room into darkness.

"Get away from the window," he hissed.

"Now wait a minute!" Susan yelled. "You have no right to...."

A bullet smashing through the window and embedding itself in the back wall silenced her.

"Get down!" he ordered.

"What the hell is going on?" Susan squirmed to remove his hand that was pressing her hard to the floor.

"We need to get out of here!"

"Get off me!" Susan snapped.

Another bullet hit the house and Charles pressed down harder. Susan pushed against him but his strength was unrelenting. In another situation, Susan may have found this exhilarating, but at the moment she was terrified. Of all the luck! Out of the twenty-three realtors who worked at Town and Country, this insane man had chosen her. She made a vow that she was never going to show another house again without some sort of background check on her buyer.

"Please believe me!"

"To go where?"

"Anywhere but here! I need your car."

"My car? Wait a minute! What's wrong with your car?"

"They shot a hole in the gas tank."

Susan hesitated. This was madness. Not only was her buyer crazy, he was also in some kind of trouble, and he'd brought the trouble right into her home. What did she know about the man other than the little bit he had told her about himself? Could she believe any of it?

The sound of men's voices coming from outside propelled her into action. She moved so suddenly she exploded out of Charles' grasp and got to her feet. Grabbing her coat and purse from the hook by the door, she ran.

Charles was right behind her.

There was no moon to help Susan and Charles work their way across her yard heading for the neighbor's property. The sound of voices coming around the side of the house was getting louder. Just as the runners were crawling past the hedge that separated the yards, one of the pursuer's flashlights swept over the area. Susan felt Charles' hand flatten her to the ground. Their bodies were so close she could tell that he was holding his breath. He kept his hand on her back until the voices faded as the intruders moved back to the front of Susan's house.

"Go!" Charles urged her as he climbed to his feet.

"Where?" she hissed.

"Take my hand," he said extending his fingers towards her. "I don't want us to get separated in the dark."

Susan glanced over her shoulder just as lights went on in her house. Momentarily stunned, she wasn't prepared for the strength of Charles' grasp or the length of his steps. Unbalanced, Susan's knees buckled and she dropped back to the ground; the forward motion of Charles' tug dragged her over the yard. Susan winced as her weight forced her knees to sink into the rough terrain, causing her to curse her early morning choice of clothing.

"Whoa!" Charles whispered. "I'm sorry. Are you hurt?"

"Scraped my knees, I think," she said thinly. She barely contained the eye roll she knew she would have been making if the situation had been safer.

"Can you walk?"

"Walk? I'm scared enough to run! Charles, I saw lights come on in my house. Who's in there?" she whispered.

"No one you'd want to meet. Let's go."

After running a short distance, he stopped. The move was so sudden Susan slammed into his back. Reaching around, Charles grabbed her upper arm and tossed her up and over his shoulder. Susan, suppressing a scream, hung on for dear life as he ran for cover behind her neighbor's hedge.

"Susan," he whispered tossing her back on her feet. "I do hope that your car keys are in the purse you're carrying."

Stabbing Charles in the chest with her finger, she hissed, "Yes, but I'm not going anywhere with you."

He grabbed her hand and squeezed. "You can't stay here!"

Susan wrenched her fingers free. "Why not? You won't tell me why men are chasing you and then you act surprised that I'm not happy to go along with whatever you say. *You* could be the person I should be running from for all I know!" her voice was rising with each word and Charles slapped a hand across her mouth. Susan's eyes burned with indignation when he refused to move his hand.

"You sure as hell can't stay here!" He dropped his hand from her face, exasperated.

"Why not? I didn't *do* anything!"

"Susan, they're in your house. They know who you are now, and you are connected to me"

Susan opened her mouth to protest but he narrowed his eyes at her. "No matter how insignificantly, they will think you know where I am. You're in as much trouble as I am."

"That's not fair," she wailed. "Can't I just tell them that I'm just an agent trying to sell you a house?"

"You think they care who you are?"

"What kind of a man are you? Why do they want to kill you?"

"This is not the time to get into that."

Susan was indignant. "Not the time? You just said that I was in as much trouble as you. If they intend to kill me just because I'm with you, don't you think I have the right to know why? Or at least the right to decide if I want to die here now or somewhere else later?"

Charles just grunted.

Susan could see the men walking from room to room in her house. The light in Julia's old bedroom went on and Susan's heart constricted. Would she ever feel safe in the house again?

"Come on, Susan. We have to get out of here!"

"How are we going to get to my car? It's in the closed garage."

"I didn't see any cars parked near your house. That means that after they hear your car start, they'll have to run to where they left their car. That gives us a little bit of time to get away. Give me the keys."

Susan opened her purse and handed the keys to Charles. "Please. Just take my car and let me stay here."

"I can't do that. They'd find you and torture you. One of their favorite tricks is pulling off fingernails. Even though you'd have no idea where I'd gone, they'd try to make you talk."

Susan glance down at her manicured nails. "Well then, m... m...maybe after we get away from here you could let me out?"

"To go where, Susan?" he asked her softly.

"I don't know, the police? Something."

Charles shook his head at her and took her hand. "Just stay with me, and I'll keep us both alive. No more questions right now."

Susan shivered.

Staying in the shadows, the two crawled toward the garage access door. Susan had never considered her backyard big, but right now the distance between them and the garage looked as long as a football field.

"There's a grouping of flowering plants on your right. Watch out for the rosebush," Susan whispered.

If a grunt meant anything, the rosebush had found him.

"Could have mentioned that a little sooner," he grumbled sourly. "Hold on while I unhook myself. My sleeve is caught on a thorn."

A rustling sound startled them.

Charles stopped in the middle of untangling his sleeve. "What was that?"

Susan could see a small creature crawling out of the foliage. "I think it's the neighbor's cat."

Charles groaned. "Susan, don't move. Don't even breathe!"

"Why Charles, it's hard to believe that you're afraid of a cat. Who would have thought…."

His whisper was guarded. "Does your neighbor's cat have a white stripe down its back?"

"Of course it doesn't!"

"It's not a cat. Stay absolutely still!"

"You're serious! Five feet away from us is a skunk?"

"You got that right!"

Light escaped from her house as the backdoor opened and a man stepped out. He looked around and seeing no one, he unzipped his pants while walking toward them.

Charles put his hand on Susan's back and flattened her to the ground again. Susan rolled her eyes; this was starting to get old.

Even though the man had stopped close to the animal, he never knew it was there until the skunk made an objection to his presence and sprayed him.

Holding their noses and trying not to gag, Susan and Charles stayed absolutely still as the man's scream brought four tough-looking men out the back door, guns drawn. They stopped abruptly when the stench hit their noses.

The sprayed man stood with his arms stuck out, not wanting to touch his own body. "Don't just stand there," he pleaded. "Help me!"

The men stayed where they were.

"Come on! Do something!" the man begged.

Other than laughing and gagging, the men turned their backs on the man and went back into the house leaving him to solve his own problem.

Using the commotion for cover, Charles and Susan crawled safely to the access door, opened it, and stood up inside the pitch-dark garage. The light that came on when the car door was opened was not seen by anyone; there were no windows in the garage. Charles silently thanked God for small favors.

"I'll turn the ignition key at the same time you hit the garage door opener. Let's get out of here while they're figuring out what to do with their smelly buddy."

Susan nodded numbly. "Have you ever been that close to a spraying skunk?" she asked.

"I can't say that I have. I didn't realize the odor was so strong! I had trouble breathing." He glanced over at her. "Susan, you have a very interesting look on your face."

Susan almost smiled. "Here I am, being chased by men who apparently want to kill me, and I'm worrying about that smelly man going into my house."

He reached over to reassure her, but instead, he sniffed.

"What?" questioned Susan.

"I'm afraid we both smell like skunk."

Susan sniffed at the sleeve of her red dress. "Oh, my goodness! You're right! How do you get rid of skunk odor?"

"You don't," Charles replied. "When we get to our destination, we'll have to ditch our clothes."

Susan's head shot up. "But this is a new dress!"

Charles waved his hand in dismissal. "We're running for our lives and you worry about a dress? Now concentrate! Make sure you know where the opener is because I'm not turning on the headlights, and you'll never find it in the dark when I close the car door. When I count to three, hit the garage door opener!"

Charles pulled the door closed, and once again, the world was pitch-black. "One, two, three."

The garage door slowly opened as the car engine sprang to life. The sprayed man was still standing in the middle of the back yard when the noise of their departure alerted those who had returned to the house. Men poured out the front door, shooting at the car as it backed out the long driveway. Charles had figured right; the men were running into the next block to find their car.

They didn't get very far before Susan's response to a bullet shattering the back window was to scream and throw herself onto the floor.

"Charles! This is madness! I want out! Just stop the car and let me go!"

"To go where?" his voice was shaking. "Back to your house? I don't think so!"

Susan sputtered. "So what am I? A hostage? Are you kidnapping me?"

Charles sighed. "I'm sorry I got you into this...I didn't have a car and I had nowhere else to go. I just had to get away from them."

"Them?" Susan yelled. "Who is 'them'?"

"Later! Would you please see if anyone is still following us?"

Susan used the sideview mirror to see behind them. "There are no lights back there."

"They could be driving with their lights off."

Susan pulled at the seat belt to hoist herself back up off the car floor. She twisted her body checking the road behind them when a bullet came through what was left of the back window and exited out through the windshield. Charles' hand shot out, grabbed her, and shoved her back to the floor.

"Stay down!" he shouted.

Charles sped up so suddenly Susan felt pinned to the floor. She lay there in utter panic. She needed to get away from the man before he got her killed. The car swerved, then went into a spin. Crammed into the small space with nothing to hold on to, Susan's head smashed into the glove box.

"For God's sake, Charles," she yelled. "This is crazy! Let me out!"

He answered her with silence. Headlights off, he continued to drive into the dark night at a speed Susan didn't even want to think about as she cowered on the floor, afraid to crawl back onto the passenger's seat.

"Stay down there!" he ordered again.

Miles flew by as she crouched on the floor. Suddenly, things changed. She watched as his foot slammed down on the brake pedal, causing the car to slide sideways. The tires were squealing on the asphalt in their attempt to keep traction. Susan screamed again.

The next sound she heard was their tires crunching gravel. When the car skidded to a complete stop, she crawled back into the passenger's seat and looked out. Charles had driven the car into a heavily wooded area. The silence after he turned off the ignition was jarring. Leaning over, he placed his fingers on her lips and left them there until the sound of cars roaring down the road they'd just exited faded.

Charles let out the breath he had been holding. "They weren't as far behind us as I thought."

The muffled sound of a ringing cell phone broke the silence. The ringtone was unfamiliar to Charles.

"Is that your cell phone?"

"Yes…it's in my purse in the backseat. Would you please reach behind and get it for me?"

His long arm had no problem retrieving the purse, but what he did next was so objectionable, Susan cried out in alarm.

"How dare you!"

"I dare, and by the way, since iPhone batteries are not removable, I thank you for not having one," Charles replied quietly as he finished removing the battery from her cell phone and sliding it into his jacket pocket.

Angry, she sputtered, "You...you...you kidnap me, risk my life...you...you...!"

"Remember when the lights came on in your house? The men involved would have ransacked your house, looking for information as to who you are, and how you're connected to me. Tell me, what would they have found?"

Susan just looked at him.

Grabbing her shoulders, he shook her. "Tell me, Susan! Talk to me! What would they have found?"

"Take your hands off me!"

His voice held a threat of violence. "I'm just going to say it one more time. What-would-they-have-found?"

Susan rubbed her shoulders. "Okay...okay! Keep your hands to yourself!"

Charles just looked at her.

"Well, the garage has real estate signs in it. The signs have my name, my e-mail address, the company that I work for, and phone numbers."

"And in the house?"

"My computer is turned on."

"Who sent you the last entry?"

"My daughter and I were messaging."

"You have a daughter?" His voice had an edge to it.

"Yes. The call you made me miss was probably from Julia." Susan's hands sat limply in her lap. *What would Julia think? Will I ever see my daughter again?*

"Damn!" Charles muttered.

"Damn? What kind of a comment is that?"

"Julia...where does she live?"

"She has an apartment near Taft School where she teaches, about twenty minutes from me. Why?"

"She could be in danger." Charles spoke so quietly, Susan had to lean her head to hear what he said.

"Danger?"

"If they think they can get a lead on where I am through you, then yes, she's in danger."

"Just because she's my daughter she's in danger? What about me?" Susan's eyes were big.

"Uh, let's just say that you're stuck with me for the time being."

"No, no, no! I have a life, I have a job! Why can't I just explain to those shooting at you that I'm just a realtor?"

His chuckle sounded rusty. "Would you be surprised to know that they really don't give a damn what you do, or who you are?"

"What kind of people are after you? They sound like animals!"

"Hmmm. I hadn't thought about them that way, but I guess they are like hungry animals. But in this case, it's not food hunger…it's money hunger."

"They're killing you for money?"

"I'm worth a lot of money dead, Susan."

"Like…like…a contract…?"

Charles nodded.

"My God, Charles! What did you do?"

"Not now, but later I'll tell you."

Susan was stunned. "Are we safe now?"

"No, we're not safe. Eventually they'll figure out that we turned off somewhere and start backtracking."

"So, what do we do?"

"Find somewhere to hide. I can't go back home, and neither can you."

"But…but," stammered Susan. "Why can't I get out here? I have friends! I can stay with them until this is all over!"

"Believe me, Susan! You can't go back home. Anyone you contact you will put in danger. Do you want to do that to your friends, your daughter? You're stuck with me whether you like it or not!"

Pounding his shoulder, she cried, "Well, I *don't* like it. This can't be happening!"

"But it is, Susan. It's happening and I don't like it any more than you do!"

"So you say!"

"I do say! Believe me, it's hard enough to stay one step ahead of them without having a whining female to contend with."

"So now I'm a whining female, am I? Well, let me tell you...."

"Susan, I don't think you understand the seriousness of the situation. I'm the only one who can keep you from getting killed. Did that word come through clearly enough? Killed."

Killed? Susan rolled that word around on her tongue. It felt strange. It also made her feel like vomiting.

Swallowing hard, she asked, "Okay, let's say that I get it. Now, how long do you figure we'll be, as you put it, stuck together?"

Charles shrugged. "I really don't know. But could we please try to be civil with each other?"

Susan thought a bit. "I guess we should at least try, but how do I know if I can trust you? I don't really know who I'm with! Are you the good guy? Or are you the bad guy?"

Charles almost chuckled. "For your sake, let's hope I'm the good guy."

CHAPTER 9

It was around 7 p.m. when, from outside, Julia heard the screaming of tires and the hysterical cries of a woman. Springing to her feet, she got to the window in time to see her neighbor, Gladys Little, standing in the middle of the street screaming and clutching a burlap bag.

* * * *

Two men were speeding away from the screaming woman they'd just pushed out of the car when the passenger's cell phone rang.

The driver barked, "Don't answer it!"

"Waddaya mean don't answer it? It's my phone, and I'm the one whose head will roll if I don't!"

"Your head is going to roll, anyway, dummy! You snatched the wrong woman!"

"Okay, so I won't answer it. What do we do now?"

"We go back and get the right one this time!"

"I think this is dumb."

"You aren't paid to think."

"Why do we have to throw a sack over her head? Whose bright idea was that?"

"You want her to be able to identify you? We just have to get her out of her apartment so one of us can be there in case her mother calls or shows up."

"So why can't we just tie her up and stash her in a closet?"

"I told you, we aren't paid to think."

By the time they returned to wait for Julia, there were several police cars parked in front of her house.

After the driver recognized the uniformed men, he grinned. "Good. Looks like Robert figured out a different way to do it."

* * * *

Mr. Little, returning home after work, was startled to see his wife standing in the middle of the street, screaming. Gladys was always screaming about something, but never in public, and certainly never in the middle of the street.

Before he managed to get his hysterical wife into his car, Julia rushed out of her house.

"Is your wife all right?"

"Uh, yes. Thanks for asking," Mr. Little answered.

"Harrumph!" Gladys snapped. "Of course I'm not all right."

"What on earth happened?"

"What happened?" Gladys cried. "I have no idea, but you do."

Julia's eyebrows went up. "I do?"

"Yes, it's you they were trying to kidnap, but they grabbed me by mistake." She waved the burlap bag. "They put this over my head so I couldn't see who they were."

Julia's face went white. "Me? Why in the world would anyone want to kidnap me?"

Gladys looked at Julia with eyes that were red from crying. "Is your mother's name Susan?"

Alarm bells went off in Julia's head. All attempts to contact her mother had failed after she had signed off to answer her doorbell. In her last message, she had written that her visitor was her Pittsburgh buyer.

Mr. Little was still trying to calm Gladys when a patrol car with two uniformed police pulled into Julia's driveway.

"Did you call the police?" Mr. Little asked Julia.

"No, I didn't, but since there're here, you'd better tell them about Gladys being kidnapped."

Julia stood to the side and watched the faces of the two officers as they listened to Gladys wild story. Every once in a while, they'd look over at her.

"Is someone going to tell me what's going on?" pleaded Julia.

Gladys snorted. "I already told you! They got really rough with me! I kept telling them that my mother has been dead for ten years, but they wouldn't believe me! But then they mentioned the name Susan, and I actually laughed at them. My mother's name was Shirley. Finally they believed me, and pushed me out of the car."

A jumble of emotions hit Julia; her knees buckled. The policeman's hands shot out and grabbed her before she hit the ground. *Mom, hadn't answered my last question when we were messaging,* Julia thought sagging further into the police officer's arm momentarily.

With a weak smile, she pushed the officer away. "I was remembering the last time I saw Mom. I was feeling so glad just to get away from her, to get back to my new life, and…and…." Julia burst into tears.

While waiting for Julia to get her emotions under control, he tried to ignore his partner who was frantically pointing at his watch.

"They'll want you at the station for questioning," he told Mr. Cook.

A puzzled Mr. Little asked, "You can't do it?"

"No, but we'll report it and someone will be calling you."

"No," Mr. Little said over his shoulder as he and his wife walked to his car. "I'm not waiting for them to call. I'm calling them as soon as I get home."

"Will they want me for questioning, too?" Julia asked.

"Yes, they will, but first let's go inside. You'll need to pack a bag, because from what Mrs. Little said, they will try again," the lead officer said.

"Wh...wh...what are you talking about? I'm not going anywhere with you. What if my mom calls? Or she comes here!"

"Miss Cook, you'll just have to trust us. Do you have any idea the danger you're in?"

"No, I don't! I know you are the police and I should trust you, but I'm not going anywhere with you until you tell me what's going on!"

"Believe me, not now! Now, get into the house and pack a bag."

"No! Tell me what's going on! Why are they looking for my mother?"

Knowing that it was just a matter of time before the real police arrived, he urged, "I'm telling you we don't have time! We've got to get you out of here, you have five minutes!"

"Why don't we have time? You're the police, aren't you? Who in their right mind would bother me when I have two policemen to protect me?"

"Enough! Into the house, Miss Cook!"

"Where am I going?"

"Somewhere safe. Probably a motel."

"We're pushing it," muttered the other cop. "We're running out of time."

Julia huffed. "I'm not paying for a motel!"

"Uh, the department will pay for it?" The younger of the two, a good-looking officer with startling blue eyes, looked for confirmation from the older one.

"Yes, yes, of course they will! Now hurry up!"

Julia resented the police who rushed her into her own house, allowing her a limited number of minutes to fill an overnight bag. How could she even think straight when the cop with the blue eyes watched her as she gathered together her underclothes? She even saw him grin when she threw several pairs of black panties onto the pile. To show him that she was aware of what he was doing, she glared at him as she dangled a black lacy bra under his nose. He quickly turned away but not before Julia got the satisfaction of seeing his red face.

She could hear the other officer on the phone, making calls to motels in the area. From what she could hear, it sounded as if someone was going to pay for her room. But for how long? And where was Mom? What kind of trouble could she have gotten herself into since Sunday? She pulled out her iPhone and tried calling again. It rang twice before she was sent straight to voicemail. Someone had to have hit the ignore button, someone had her mother's phone, and worse they probably had her mother.

"Are you about ready, Miss Cook? We need to get you out of here."

"Are we going to the station first? You said they wanted me there for questioning."

"Uh," the blue-eyed one looked to his partner for help. "We can do that after we get you settled. Now hurry up!"

"I'm allowed to have my car, aren't I? And what about work?"

"One thing at a time. First, let's get you settled, and then we'll see. If we can find your mother, this whole thing could be settled, and you'll be back here before you know it."

Julia took one last look around, and then followed the officers out the door.

CHAPTER 10

Dennis Senior carried his cell phone out the side door and onto the deck. With his back to the house, he hunched his shoulders, held the phone close to his ear, and whispered into it. Denny shook his head as he watched him through the window. There he was, doing it again. Long ago, he had given up trying to find out who his dad talked to, who he worked for, and where he went at night when he thought he was sneaking out. What kind of job had hours like that? Whoever employed his dad must be pleased with his work because there never was a shortage of money.

After his mother had walked out on them when he was nine, Dennis had tried, but Denny had serious doubts about his dad's parenting skills. In fact, Denny had found a book one day when he was searching for an envelope. His dad had hidden "Dummies' Guide to Single Parenthood" in his desk drawer.

Denny watched as his dad yelled something into his cell phone, put the phone in his pocket and headed for the garage. The sound of tires screeching as he exited the garage wasn't an unusual thing to hear. His dad had a hot temper and he did nothing to curb it. Denny had figured out that it was his dad's very effective controlling tool.

Without his dad in it, the house seemed very quiet. Denny shrugged, went to his room, and with complete concentration, planned the next week's lessons for his eighth graders. Thinking about school made him think about the very pretty Julia Cook. He knew that eventually she would have learned that he still lived at home, but why did it have to happen before she even got to know him? Now she would look at him with different eyes. He sighed. What was done was done.

He couldn't help wondering what Julia was doing right this minute. Did she have a boyfriend? That was a silly thought. Of course, she had a boyfriend! Any girl as pretty as she was certainly had a boyfriend…maybe several.

With a shrug of his shoulders, he called for his dog. Roscoe needed exercise and since it was too dark for him to chase the ball, they'd just take a walk.

They were standing under a streetlight when Julia's red convertible drove by. Since she was clutching the wheel and staring straight ahead, she never saw Denny. Noticing the police car in the front of her and a police car behind her, Denny wondered if Julia was being escorted, or was it just a coincidence?

CHAPTER 11

For the next ten minutes, Susan and Charles sat in the dark car, wondering if they were really safe. Were the bad guys still around, just waiting for them to start the car and show themselves?

Finally, Charles stirred. "Maybe we're safe, and maybe we're not. Let's find out."

He turned the key.

The loud sound of the starting engine shattered the silence. Susan frowned. "I hope they aren't close enough to hear that!"

Charles nodded his head in agreement. "Susan, where does this road go?"

"I don't know where we are. Remember, I spent most of the time on the floor. Do you have a destination in mind?"

"Yes, I do, but it would help if I knew where we are now."

"I have a GPS. Would that help?"

He nodded. "It sure would!"

She gave him a dirty look. "It's on my cell phone, and you took the battery out…remember?"

"Oh."

"Oh? Is that all you have to say?"

Charles didn't say anything for a few seconds. "You have to understand that the people who are involved in finding me are very sophisticated. They have the ability to trace calls, and that's why I don't have a cell phone, and that's why I took your battery."

"Oh."

He chuckled. "Oh? Is that all you have to say?"

"You could have told me the reason when you took it. As it was, you just scared the hell out of me."

Charles reached out and patted her hand. "For that, I apologize."

"Well, for your information, I'm still scared."

He paused for a moment before he said quietly, "So am I."

Susan shuddered. "Knowing that doesn't make me feel any better. So, what do we do now?"

"I suppose it would take time for them to find the information that they would need to trace your phone. The next question is do we take a chance that they haven't as yet put a tracer on your cell and turn it on?"

"Maybe if we didn't spend too much time, they wouldn't have a chance to trace my phone. I watch crime shows, too, you know."

Charles reached into his pocket and pulled out the battery.

With skilled fingers, she inserted the battery and turned on the phone.

"Tell me the destination and I'll type it in."

"2915 Woodland."

Susan's head rose. "Here in town?"

"Just outside town. Don't waste time! Just do it!"

She touched the map icon, typed in the address, and waited. The map appeared, showing where they were in relation to 2915 Woodland. Charles studied it, and then said, "Turn it off, and give me the battery."

Putting the car into drive, he pulled out of their hiding place and back onto the gravel road.

"Aren't you going to turn on the lights? How can you see to drive?"

"I want to get a bit further away from the main road. They could be driving up and down trying to find the side road we turned on."

Slowly he drove a mile in the dark before he turned on the headlights. They didn't say a word to each other as the car's bright headlights cut holes through the inky blackness of the night.

It had been such a pleasant day until she opened the door, and right out of Pandora's box, there was Charles. Glancing over at him for assurance, the sight of his rigid posture that was radiating anxiety was not comforting; he was just as scared as she was. She'd bet that if she could see his hands gripping the wheel, his knuckles would be white. He was also having trouble seeing through the shattered windshield. Cold air blowing in from the holes in the back window made her wish she had grabbed a warmer coat when they'd run out of her house.

Without taking his eyes off the road, Charles said, "Turn up the heat if you're cold."

"I was just wishing I'd grabbed a different coat."

"I'll find a warmer coat for you when we get to Woodland."

"You own the house on Woodland?" Susan took a deep breath when the realization hit her. Twisting her body, she confronted him. "Hey, wait a minute! You *did* have a place to go when they were chasing you. Why didn't you go to Woodland instead of getting me involved in your mess?"

"My car ran out of gas. Remember? Anyhow, we'll have a safe place to spend the night."

"W...w...we're spending the night together?"

Charles looked at her in disbelief. "We're running for our lives and you're worried about our sleeping arrangements? We won't be there very long."

"We won't?"

"You're just going to have to trust me. I'm doing the best to keep us both alive."

She gulped for air. "Good God!" she exclaimed.

Charles almost smiled. "Are you swearing or praying?"

She sighed. "You'll have to excuse me, but knowing that someone wants to harm me, a widowed real estate agent, is a new concept. Maybe my life was unexciting before I answered the door today, but at least I wasn't being scared out of my wits!"

Charles reached over and took her hand.

Fifteen minutes of silence later, he pulled onto a long dirt road that eventually dead-ended at a house.

Like a gentleman, Charles opened Susan's car door and helped her out to stand on shaky legs.

"Sorry about your car," he muttered.

Susan shrugged. "At least we're still alive."

Placing his hand under her elbow, he led her up the short path to the porch. "Careful now. There are four steps."

It was hard to see in the dark, but the house appeared to be a two-story colonial. She could see the outline of a much larger building beyond the house.

"We're here."

From a ring of keys, he produced one that fit into the lock, and with one turn, he pushed open the door and led her into the dark. A musty smell hit her nose.

"You haven't been here in a while, have you?" she asked.

"Whoooeee." He wrinkled his nose. "Maybe if we open some windows ...."

Susan had already started on the window over the sink. No matter how hard she tried, the window stayed closed.

Pushing her aside, he said, "Here, let me try."

The window didn't budge. "I guess it's been painted shut too many times. Let's try another."

Caught off guard when Charles suddenly turned and bumped into her, she lost her balance and would have again landed on her butt if his arms hadn't caught her before she hit the floor.

Flustered, she bristled at first, but then the feel of strange arms around her became exciting; the urge to nestle against his body was strong. Feeling her indecision, his arms pulled her closer. For a moment, she relaxed...and then she stiffened her body and pushed him away.

Seeing her reaction, he muttered, "Sorry!"

When she mumbled something that he didn't hear, Charles was afraid to ask her to repeat it.

After a few windows were opened and cold air rushed in, the house did smell better, but the chilly air had her rubbing goosebumps off her arms.

"Cold?" asked Charles.

"A bit," she admitted. "You did say you were going to give me a warmer coat once we got here."

"I will, but not until we get rid of our clothes. Any coat you'd put on over your smelly ones would pick up the skunk scent."

Susan gave him a quizzical look. "You probably have clothes in the closet to put on after we ditch the skunky ones. But what about me? Do you have any female clothes that some lady friend of yours left behind?"

"Nice try, Susan. But, no, I don't have any lady dresses. All I have for you is a sweatsuit that shrank several sizes the first time I washed it. As for underwear, I can offer you a clean pair of my shorts."

Susan rolled her eyes. "Well, give me a plastic bag to put my beautiful new red dress and my underclothes in, hand me your shrunken sweatsuit and a pair of your shorts, and point me to the shower. Do you have any tomato juice in case our hair smells like skunk?"

Charles stepped closer and buried his nose in her hair. "All I smell is shampoo and hair spray."

"Thank goodness," Susan sighed.

Charles led her upstairs to the guest room, and after giving her a plastic bag and his old sweatsuit and shorts, left her to shower. He disappeared into the master bedroom.

Later, smelling much better, Susan was downstairs inspecting the kitchen when Charles joined her.

"Hungry?" he asked.

Susan shrugged and leaned on the counter. "Not really. Are you?"

His eyes took in the domestic scene and found it breathtaking. Susan looked completely right in his kitchen. The blue of his sweatsuit matched her eyes, the rolled up pant legs gave her a casual, homey look, and the wet hair that hung to her shoulders made her look like a teenager.

"Charles?"

"Oh." He shook his head as if to wake himself up. "No. I can wait for breakfast."

"Have you forgotten about the coat? I'm a little chilly."

With a sly grin on his face, he went to a closet and stopped. "I'm going to show you a very special coat, but first I'm going to tell you the story behind it. It was a gift from Tig…uh, it was a gift from a fellow golfer."

"A fellow golfer? You play golf?"

"Uh, you might say I used to."

"A gift for what?"

"Well, it was a joke-gift. I don't like to play golf when it's cold. One spring, it started to snow when we were halfway through a tournament and I complained…a lot. The coat was presented to me at the awards dinner."

"Did everyone laugh?"

He grinned. "They did. I got a lot of ribbing, but in the end, I won because I kept the coat."

Pulling it out of the closet, he turned to Susan. "Take the coat. You can use it as a blanket."

The coat he was offering Susan was huge. The dense fur shimmered in the light, the browns and blacks melted into one color, and the white fur trim was breathtaking. The enormity of the garment stole her breath.

"Wow!" she whispered.

"Take it," Charles urged.

"Wow!" Susan repeated. "A lot of animals gave their lives for this coat! Tell me, what kind of fur is the white trim?"

"Ermine." Charles chuckled. "I can see that you're impressed. Just wait until you feel the weight of it." With that, he draped the coat over her arm.

Susan staggered. "Wow! It's heavy! And look! It's a fur coat lined with fur!"

"Yeah. The story is that the coat was especially made for a very large Alaskan billionaire who died before he paid for it. When his widow refused to follow through with the purchase, Tig...ah, a golfer made an offer the furrier couldn't refuse." He looked at his watch. "It's too late to do anything tonight. We'll stay here until the sun comes up, so find a bed. I know I'm going to try to get some shut-eye because I don't like to fly when I'm tired."

Susan's eyes flew open. "Fly?"

The word seemed to hang in the air. The very pretty woman was looking at him with disbelief on her face.

"Yes, fly."

She sputtered. "You're telling me that tomorrow morning we're going to get on a plane and fly somewhere?"

"What's the problem? Something wrong with flying? We sure as hell can't stay here!"

"And I suppose the plane is right outside just waiting for us?" The sarcasm in her voice matched her face.

"That's right."

Her eyes opened wide. "Now you're scaring me!"

The expression on his face softened. "Again, I apologize. I never should have gotten you into my mess, but what's done is done. Both of us should be scared."

"And... and... this plane that you say is outside...you fly it?"

Charles chuckled. "If you're looking for the word that describes someone who flies a plane, the word is *pilot,* Susan."

She waved him off. "I know that, and you know that I know that! This is no time to be funny! So, are you the pilot?"

He nodded. "It's my plane. I've been flying for years."

"And these men who are trying to kill you, they don't know anything about this place or your plane?"

"Not yet."

"Does your wife know about this place?" Surprised that she'd asked that, Susan's hand flew to her mouth.

Without a sound, his face changed. Turning away from her, he went to the foot of the stairs where he stopped. Staring straight ahead, he answered,

"We've talked enough. Feel free to take any of the rooms upstairs…except the one I'm in, of course. I'll wake you at dawn."

With her mouth hanging open, she watched her captor disappear up the stairs.

CHAPTER 12

Julia glanced out the motel window. Her car wasn't there. Had they taken her car away so that she couldn't leave the motel? How dare they! She had worked herself up to an explosive level when she was surprised by the sound of a muffled ringing phone. Frantically looking for it, she finally found it under a pillow.

"Hello?" she asked in a hesitant voice. Who would be calling her? Who knew she was here?

"Miss Cook?" Julia recognized the voice of one of the officers. "Your car has been moved to the back of the motel."

Julia took a deep breath, and as she exhaled, all the pent-up anger over the belief that the officers had taken her car away disappeared, leaving her feeling empty.

"Oh," she said in a small voice.

"Yeah, that red convertible is a sweet car, but it's too noticeable."

"So, can I use it? There's really no kitchen in the room other than a coffee pot, so what am I supposed to eat? Can I go to work?"

"Uh, we'll have to get back to you on that, as for the food, something will be arranged."

"Really? I thought you said I had to go to the station to answer some questions. When is that going to happen?"

"Uh, later."

Julia shrugged. "So I'm supposed to sit in this room until you give me permission to leave it?"

"I'm glad you understand. Bye."

Julia was left with a silent phone and an open mouth.

* * * *

The man with the icy blue eyes nodded his approval. "It wasn't a good idea to have her red convertible in front of the motel for the whole world to see. Lord knows who may come looking for her when she doesn't show up for work tomorrow."

* * * *

Denny drove slowly through the school's parking lot, checking the cars already there. He was concerned when he didn't see the red convertible. Running through his mind was the memory of seeing Julia last night when she drove under the streetlight sandwiched between two cop cars. He shook the thought out of his head. No way. It had just been a coincidence. It took a quick glance at his watch to turn his thoughts back to the present problem; if he wanted to get to his classroom before the bell rang, he had to run.

Maybe if he hadn't bumped into a heavy-set woman on his rush to his room, he might have made it. As it was, he was courteous enough to stop and act contrite.

"I'm so sorry!" he apologized, his face red.

"Humph," the woman muttered.

"Are you okay?" he asked.

She looked at him over the rim of her glasses. "The kids aren't allowed to run in the hall, but the teachers are?"

Denny was speechless until he saw the twinkle in her eyes.

"Teachers are allowed to run if they're going to be late for their class."

"It's good to know that," she grinned. "By the way, I'm Hazel McGregor. Do you know where Miss Cook's room is? I'm her sub today."

"Oh." Denny looked surprised. "Did she call in sick?"

"No, she didn't. But when it looked like Miss Cook was either running late or not coming at all, Mrs. Sheldon was just lucky that I was in the building this morning. I had just dropped in to pick up my bag of goodies that I left here the last time I subbed."

So Julia wasn't coming to work today. Maybe her being sandwiched between two cop cars wasn't a coincidence after all. Realizing Mrs. McGregor was waiting for an answer, Denny pointed. He could already hear riotous noise coming out of Julia's room. "You might have your hands full today, Mrs. McGregor! It sounds like they're ready to pounce on any substitute who walks through that door."

"Not on this sub they won't!"

By the time Denny got to his own classroom, there was not a peep coming from Julia's room. *I wonder how she did that,* he thought.

Upon opening the door to his room, his ears were assaulted by the racket. He stopped long enough to catch his breath before he strode to the front of the room trying to look as if he were in command; the noise continued.

He'd give anything to know Mrs. McGregor's secret.

CHAPTER 13

After a very long and sleepless night, Julia had had it. How dare they deposit her in this crummy motel. She remembered the officer who had spent time on the phone calling around to the different motels in town. No doubt he had chosen the cheapest of the lot. There had been only one packet of coffee for the machine in the room; she had emptied that pot hours ago. Her empty stomach rumbled. If her captors weren't going to feed her, then screw them! Grabbing her coat and purse, she stuck her head out the door, and seeing no one, she slipped out and quietly closed the door behind her.

Heading for the back of the motel where the officer had said he had parked her car, she was rounding the side of the building when she heard voices. Were her policemen coming to check on her? She stopped, pressed her body close to the building, and waited.

"You think this is the right motel?"

"Yeah, that's her red convertible."

"You sure this is the right way to do this? Couldn't we just talk to her here at the motel?"

"We have our orders! If her mother had showed up at Julia's apartment, we wouldn't have to do this. She says she doesn't know where her mother is, but we need to make sure she's telling the truth."

The man chuckled. "And I've seen the way you make people tell the truth!"

Julia gasped. The second voice was familiar, but it wasn't the voice of either of the police officers.

Julia had to know. Peeking around the corner, she saw Denny and two tough- looking men walking in her direction. What in the world was Denny doing here? Had the principal, Mrs. Sheldon, sent him to look for her? That didn't make sense. He had his own classroom to take care of.

As she was about to step out and greet him, the familiar voice spoke. "When you grab her, I hope she doesn't make as much noise as that other dame."

Grab her?

"You aren't doing this one?" asked an unfamiliar voice.

"No, not this time," she heard Denny say. "I'll do the bag thing, but I don't want her to see me."

One of the men snickered. "Are you getting shy in your old age?"

"I just don't want her to be able to identify me after all this is over. I've met her. She and my son teach at the same school."

Julia gasped. Denny's dad? Denny's dad was mixed up in this mess? Willing her feet to move didn't work; they were paralyzed.

The sound of a car pulling up to the front of the motel put her suddenly unparalyzed feet into motion, and the next thing she knew she was running for her life toward the car. It was only after she had reached it, opened the door, and threw herself onto the floor did she become aware that it was a police car.

The surprised officer blinked. "Well, good morning to you, too!"

Panting from the short sprint, Julia looked up into the icy blue eyes of the young cop who had admired her black panties. "Don't look down at me! Pretend I'm not here! Just go!"

"Wh... wh... what?"

"Just go! There are three men back there looking for my car!"

The surprised look on the officer's face stayed frozen as he drove away from the motel. Julia was taken aback by the panic in his voice when he asked, "Did you recognize anyone?"

Why was he so fearful that she might have recognized someone? Julia thought hard before she answered, "No."

With a relieved smile, he said, "Of course you wouldn't have recognized them. Miss Cook, you have a wild imagination!"

Puzzled, Julia tilted her head, squinted her eyes, and studied the officer. Something wasn't right. "What in the world do you mean by that?"

"I noticed when I moved your car to the back of the lot that one of the tires was almost flat. The men that you heard were trying to find your car to fix the tire."

"Really?"

"Yes, really! I do a good job of taking care of those who are put in my charge for protection. The last thing you need is a flat tire when it's time for you to leave."

Julia opened her mouth, and then she closed it. Why would he make up such a wimpy excuse for the three men? She would keep quiet about the fact that she knew one of them until she had a chance to figure out what was going on.

What kind of mess had her mother gotten into? She stayed on the floor of the squad car, wondering how safe she was riding around with the blue-eyed officer who made up stories. Why was he so concerned that she might have recognized one of them? The fact that she knew that Dennis Senior wanted to grab her was disturbing. What would have happened if she'd told the blue-eyed officer that, in fact, she did know one of the men?

"Sir?" she called up to him. She watched his face, and seeing no reaction, repeated herself. "Sir?"

Muttering to himself, and gripping the wheel, the officer was deep in thought.

"SIR!" Julia yelled.

"Wh... wh... what?" he roared. "Jeez, you scared me!"

"Sorry about that, but I need to know who you are. What's your name?"

"My name? You scare the shit out of me just to ask me my name?"

"I said I was sorry."

The officer caught his breath and relaxed. "I'm Officer Robert Fox."

"Robert", Julia repeated. "Does anyone ever call you Officer Bob?"

"No, they don't. You may call me Robert if you like, but I don't answer to the name Bob."

"Got it. Okay, Officer Robert, where are we going?"

"I haven't figured that one out."

"If the men that I saw were there just to fix my tire, why can't I go back to my room at the motel?" Julia watched as a myriad of expressions crossed his face. Still crouched on the floor of the car, Julia watched the street lights as they passed. A funny thought that Robert should never take up the game of poker flew through her head and then disappeared as fast as it came.

Robert squirmed. "Well, that is, uh, let's not do that."

"Why? If those men were from some garage, why should that change anything?"

"B...b...because," he hesitated, and then he beamed, "because I didn't see them, so I can't be sure they were from the garage!"

Julia frowned. If Officer Robert had spelled a word right in a spelling bee contest, he couldn't have looked more pleased with himself. Something was wrong.

She turned her body so that he couldn't see her fumbling in her purse for her cell phone. Who could she call? The fact was that she was so new in the city, she had no one but Denny; calling him could be the biggest mistake she might ever make. Dare she call 911? And tell them what? Some rouge cop kidnapped her? No, that wasn't such a good idea, either. Deep in thought, the ringing of her phone startled her.

"Hello?" she questioned.

"Julia, oh, thank God!"

Julia squealed, "Mom?"

"Don't say anything, just let me talk!"

"But Mom!"

"Listen! I'm in trouble! You know my Pittsburgh buyer? He showed up at my house last night being chased by men who have a contract to kill him! We escaped. Right now, we're at his house only God knows where, and he says that he has a plane and is going to fly us to a safe place! I'm scared out of my wits! He took the battery out of my cell so that it couldn't be traced, but he went outside without his jacket, and I grabbed my battery out of a pocket so that I could call you. He said you might be in trouble, too, if they think you might know where I am. Oh, here he comes...." The phone went dead. Julia had never heard her mother so frantic and out of control before.

"So who called? Your face is white."

Julia shuddered. "Oh, no one, uh, no one."

"Liar! I heard you say 'Mom'. Why are you lying?"

"Why should you care if I'm lying, and it's none of your business anyway!"

Office Robert slammed on the brakes, pulled over to the curb, and grabbed the phone out of her hand.

"Wait a minute! Who said you could take my phone?" Julia was off the floor, grabbing at her phone.

Officer Robert's fist shot out and caught her chin. Julia crumpled back to the floor.

He pulled out his own phone and hit speed dial. "I got her," he said to someone. "And better yet, I have her phone. Her mother just called." He listened. "Uh, what is she doing right now? Well, I had to knock some sense into her, so right now she's not doing anything. And yes, I'll bring her in."

CHAPTER 14

Julia woke with a start. Where was she? And why was it so hard to sit up? The only light in the small windowless room came from a bare bulb that hung on a cord from the ceiling. Her jaw hurt, but for some reason, she couldn't touch it. What was wrong with her hands? Memory was slow in coming, but when it came back, the horror of her situation forced her to lay her head back on the floor; her hands were tied, and her feet were duct-taped together.

Julie heard a door open and close in the adjoining room.

"...so, then I hit her. I really didn't mean to knock her out!"

"You did good, Bob."

"How many times do I have to tell you my name is Robert?"

Julia's eyes flew open. She recognized the voices of the two cops who had taken her to the motel.

"Whatever. Were they able to trace the phone?"

"Yes, and I just heard from one of the guys who was sent to do away with the golfer and the real estate lady. According to him, we can consider it done. They're both dead. Wouldn't it be nice if there had been a price on the lady, too?"

"So if both of them are dead, we don't need the daughter anymore."

Julia gasped. Her mom was dead?

Robert's voice replied, "She wouldn't have been any help, anyway. She didn't know where her mother was, but her phone knew!"

Tears were streaming down Julia's face. Waves of abject fear, anger, and grief overwhelmed her. When her insides cramped and turned to water, her stomach and bowls emptied themselves. As she scooted to a dry spot on the floor, she wailed. She was never going to see her mom again.

"You did a great thing when you grabbed her phone. If I were you, I'd ask for a bonus."

Bonus? Dirty cops, Julia thought to herself.

"Honest to God, it was like a miracle!" laughed the man Julia knew as Officer Robert. "There I was, waiting for them to bring her with a bag over her head, and then all of a sudden, there she is on the floor of my car! I couldn't believe my luck! But since our job is finished, we don't need her anymore."

"But she knows what we look like! Especially you!"

"We'll be so far away she won't be able to finger us. I say we cut her loose and drop her off on some isolated road. Someone is bound to come along and give her a ride."

"Do you really think we should take the chance?"

"Well, what's the alternative? Kill her?"

Julia held her breath.

It was Officer Robert's voice that said, "Hey, I got into this for the money. Killing people was not part of the deal."

Julia heard a snicker.

Robert snorted. "Don't laugh at me! I'm not doing it. If you think it's the right thing to do, then you do it."

No matter how hard Julia strained, she couldn't hear what the other cop's reply. Had he said that he would do it? Had he said he would kill her?

When she heard footsteps coming closer to her door, she closed her eyes and lay very still. She held her breath as the footsteps stopped on the other side of her door. Whoever it was, he remained there for several minutes. By the time she heard his footsteps retreating, her lungs were begging for air. With no way to judge the passing of time, she lay for hours shivering on the dirty floor, trying to make sense out of what was happening. How could her saintly mother get herself into so much trouble? Thinking about the bonus Robert should get for grabbing her phone, she remembered that her mother had said that there was a contract to kill her Pittsburgh buyer. Her realtor mom was getting herself killed because of a buyer. Then, her thoughts went to her classroom. Was anyone wondering why she hadn't shown up for work? Mrs. Sheldon would think that she was irresponsible for not calling in sick and asking for a substitute. Just the thought that she might lose her job brought more tears. That other eighth-grade teacher must be wondering where she was. Thinking of Denny McCain brought his dad to her mind. Did Denny know that his dad was involved in this whole mess…whatever the mess was?

Her empty stomach growled, her full bladder complained, her pants were soiled, her wrists were rubbed raw, and her mouth tasted like vomit.

It was dangerously quiet in the other room.

CHAPTER 15

Susan stood at the window and watched as the big overhead door of the out- building rolled up. Dawn hadn't completely made its appearance, although the sky to the east was showing promising signs. It was too dark to see inside the building, but she knew Charles was there; she had seen him go in.

Missing her toothbrush and cosmetics, Susan was feeling uneasy with her body. Charles had promised that she'd be able to replace everything when they landed. Where that was, he wouldn't say. Until then , his sweatsuit was comfortable enough, although she couldn't say the same about his shorts. Her shoes had escaped the skunk's wrath, and for that, she was thankful.

When a light went on in the out building, Susan got her first glimpse of a small plane. Several beat-up cars shared the space, and Susan watched as Charles drove her car into the building to join the others.

The pantry had plenty of canned goods so Susan couldn't complain about being hungry. This morning Charles had taken over the kitchen detail and after making coffee, he'd heated up a can of pork and beans and a can of corn. Susan had been too upset to eat very much.

Now standing looking out at the world that was getting lighter, her stomach growled. Her attention was pulled back to the building just in time to see a small plane that looked like it could hold no more than two people being pushed out. After Charles pulled the door down on the building and locked it, he turned and walked toward the house.

"Ready?" he called to her.

Susan didn't bother to answer. Ready for what?

Charles joined her in the house. "I'll just check to make sure all the lights have been turned off, and then we'll go."

"Go where?" she asked again.

"That's information you don't need to know."

Susan stamped her foot, but a look from Charles made her keep her mouth shut. Grabbing the fur-lined fur coat, she left the house and headed toward the waiting plane.

From high in the sky, Charles looked down at the house they had just left. After a quick intake of breath and a muttered curse, he straightened the plane, pulled on the controls, and headed for a higher altitude.

Susan looked over at him, a question in her eyes.

"Tell me you didn't!" he yelled at her over the noisy engine.

"Didn't what?" she yelled back.

"Call someone."

Susan stuck out her chin. "What if I did?"

"You almost got us killed! Look out the window."

Susan leaned over, looked out the window, and gasped. Men were spilling out of cars that were lining up in front of the house they'd just left. While Charles circled in the sky, they watched the house being torched.

"Charles, I...I...I'm so sorry! It was just a really short call to my daughter! I knew she must be *so* worried ...."

Charles didn't reply. All she could see of him was his stony profile as he made one large circle over his burning property, his fingers clenched tightly on the controls. The men setting the fire looked up to see a plane speeding down toward them. Seeing their terrified faces almost made

Charles smile; instead, he pulled back on the joystick and headed for higher altitude.

Susan sighed. She was the cause of the fire down there that had already included his barn. Thinking of all the cars in that barn, hers included, she reached over and touched his shoulder. "I'm so sorry, Charles," she began. He shook off her hand.

For a few seconds, she felt tremendous guilt for being the one responsible for the destruction of his property, but the guilt passed when she reasoned that she was here, fleeing for her life, because he had knocked on her door, and brought his problems to her.

Since she hadn't slept too well last night, maybe sleeping would be the best way to stay out of trouble. Her eyes were closing when she felt the coat being thrown over her. She didn't bother to open them.

* * * *

Susan was dreaming of a sunny day at the beach with her husband and baby Julia. The sky was blue, the sand was hot, and the love of her life was lying beside her. Could it get any better than this? Her husbands hand was gently shaking her shoulder. Turning towards him, he morphed. It was a slow change, like watching ice cream melt. Instead of her husband's dark chestnut hair and crooked smile, Charles Holiday stared at her. He shook her harder and she pushed his hand away.

"For God's sake, Susan, wake up!" Charles yelled.

"Wh... wh... what?" Susan shot upright, as if she had been falling. Her eyes found Charles and what she saw there was not comforting.

"We're in trouble! Are you belted?"

Susan fumbled around, found the belt, and gave it a tug. "Yes, I am. What's going on, Charles?"

He didn't say anything, just pointed. Even though Susan had never before seen a plane's instrument panel, she knew that all the indicators shouldn't be glowing red. The engine was sputtering with long periods of silence between sputters.

"What do we do? Oh, my God," Susan howled. "We're going to crash!"

"Look down and spot a place to land!" Charles barked.

Susan looked down and saw only heavily forested areas where trees were already showing tinges of Autumn coloring.

"Do you see a road? I can land this thing on a road."

"There's no road! Where in the hell are we?" Susan cried.

Charles didn't answer. He had seen a clearing large enough to land his plane. With one final cough, the engine went silent. Neither spoke as the plane went into a rapid descent.

At the end, Charles yelled, "Brace yourself!"

And then blackness consumed her.

CHAPTER 16

Susan woke to a strange world. Why would she be strapped to a chair in the lower branches of a tree? And why the strong smell of gasoline? Dazed, she looked down. Her eyes fell on the wreckage of the small plane and the horror of it all came back to her. She and Charles had crashed. He had indeed found a small clearing in the vast ocean of trees, but it hadn't been big enough. She was still stunned, but the sight of smoke coming out of the wreckage was enough to spring her into action.

Charles.

Where was Charles? Was he alive? Frantically she tried to separate herself from the chair. The fur coat that had made it out of the plane with her was now interfering with her frantic attempt to remove the belt. Her fingers didn't want to work. Charles! Where was Charles? Was he dead? Oh, God! What was she going to do if Charles was dead?

Whimpering and praying while she fumbled, she wasn't prepared when removing the strap freed her body; she tumbled the short distance to the ground.

She lay still, examining her body. When nothing appeared to be broken or hurt, she shook her head in wonder. Had she survived a plane crash and a fall from a tree without being injured? But what about Charles? Her nose was stinging from gasoline fumes and smoke. She knew that if Charles were still in the plane, he had to be rescued before it exploded. Cautiously she picked herself off the ground, waiting for some part of her body to complain, or worse, not work. When her first tentative steps assured her that she was uninjured, she rushed to the pilot's side of the plane dreading what she might see.

Charles, his head bloody, was draped over the controls. Her pulling, tugging, and praying had no effect on the caved-in door.

Charles wasn't moving.

"Don't you dare die on me!" she screamed.

She fought to open the door until her nails were broken and her fingers were bloody. Her howling cries shifted from praying for strength, to railing at God for not helping, and at Charles for getting her into this mess. Finally, using strength that surprised her, one last frantic effort opened the door, throwing her off balance. Flat on the ground where she landed, she could see into the cockpit. There he was, his head covered in blood, all six feet of him and probably two hundred pounds of dead weight, waiting to be rescued.

Scrambling to her feet, she heaved his body off the controls and started to work on the seatbelt. His body kept toppling back over the controls, and by the time she managed to remove the seatbelt, she was panting.

Getting the belt off him had been difficult, but it was nothing compared to the strain of pulling his long body out of the cockpit. By dragging it for four steps and resting, and then another four and resting, she was lying exhausted beside his still form when with a whoosh, the plane exploded with such intense heat the nearby trees were singed.

Charles stirred.

"You're alive! Oh, thank God!"

He moaned.

"Charles! Charles!" she cried. "Please open your eyes!"

He turned his head toward the sound of her voice. Slowly, his eyes opened, and at the sight of Susan, a slow smile spread across his face.

While attempting to sit up, his arms encircled a surprised Susan and pulled her down on top of him. "Well, hello there!" he grinned. "Aren't you a pretty one!"

Surprised, she pushed him away, removed his arms, and skidded out of his reach.

"Hey, don't be like that!" he pouted.

"Cut it out!" Susan spoke harshly. "I need to know how badly you're hurt."

He looked puzzled. "I'm hurt? Why would I be hurt?"

"Come on now! Our plane just crashed!"

"Our plane? We have a plane?"

"Well, we did. It just blew up...see the wreckage over there?" She pointed to the smoldering wreckage.

"Oh, that's bad!" Charles frowned. "So, where's the pilot?"

"Quit playing around! You know very well that you were flying the plane!"

He threw back his head and laughed. "Then no wonder we crashed! I have no idea how to fly a plane."

She panicked. Was she stranded in a place that only God knew where with a man who wasn't rational? Not wanting him to be alarmed, she spoke quietly. "I'm going to ask you to do something."

He grinned. "Does this 'something' have anything to do with you and me, darlin'? And I must say, that over-sized sweatsuit you have on doesn't really hide what I'm interested in. Come a little closer and I'll show you."

Susan scooted further away from him. "Take a hand and feel your head."

He laughed. "Is this some kind of game?"

She shook her head. "Just do it."

"Okay, I'll play your silly game!"

His grin disappeared when his hand encountered a wet and sticky substance.

"What the hell?" he frowned.

"Look at your hand, Charles."

"You have to quit that, you know."

"Quit what?"

"Calling me Charles. That's not my name...hey! Why is my hand bloody?"

"I'm calling you Charles because that's your name, and your hand is bloody because you touched your head."

His eyes widened. "I'm bleeding? Why am I bleeding?"

With a feeling that all was lost, Susan groaned.

Scanning his surroundings for a familiar face, Charles turned back to her. "Tell me the truth, pretty lady. Did my golfing buddies put you up to this?"

"No, this is no joke. Let's talk about your name. If you say it's not Charles, then what is it?"

"Why, Ryan Wilcox, of course! Everyone knows my name!"

"Really? And why would everyone know your name?"

He looked at her with squinted eyes. "You're putting me on, aren't you?"

"No, I'm not! Why should I know your name?"

"Because I'm famous! And you," he cocked his head and looked at her closely, "...hmmm. I don't know. If you weren't so old, I'd say you were a groupie."

Susan sputtered. "A groupie?"

"Yeah, you know, the eager girls who hang around famous people hoping to be noticed?"

"And you have lots of them?"

He grinned. "What do you think?"

Think? It was hard to think under these conditions, but floating to the surface of her mind was a vague memory of a golfer who'd disappeared under mysterious circumstances about ten years ago. A bump on his head made him think he was Ryan Wilcox?

The sun was setting and in the deep woods, she knew that it would get dark soon. She couldn't remember what date it was, but she knew it was after Thanksgiving. Since Charles wouldn't tell her where they were going, she had no idea what direction the plane had been flying; she just hoped it hadn't been north. Remembering the heavy fur coat, she glanced back and was relieved to see that it was dangling from the chair that was still wedged in the tree.

"Ryan, I need to look at your head to see where all that blood is coming from. Will you promise not to grab me when I do?"

"Aw, you're no fun!" he complained. "Okay, I promise."

Without water or cloths, she had no idea how she was going to clean his head. There had been first aid equipment on the plane, but that had burned along with everything else. The helplessness of their situation was finally sinking in. Nobody knew where they were. She sure didn't, and she'd bet her last dollar that Charles wouldn't remember either. Her phone. She could put the battery back in her cell and call for help.

"Char...Ryan! Give me the battery to my cell, please!"

There was a blank look on his face. "You want a battery for what?"

"My cell phone! I can call for help!"

"I have no idea what you're talking about!"

"Look. Reach into your right jacket pocket and give me what's in there."

Obediently, he rolled over, found his pocket, and stuck his hand in.

"This is what you want?" he asked as he passed it to her.

Susan had already pulled her phone out of her jacket pocket.

"That's a funny little thing you have there. You call it a cell?" he asked.

Susan was too busy putting the battery in to answer.

Then, with a cry of despair, she sank to the ground.

There was no service available.

CHAPTER 17

Denny paced around the office until Mrs. Sheldon hung up the phone.

"You need to speak with me?" she asked.

"I notice that the sub for Miss Cook's room was here again today."

"Yes, she was. I was lucky to get her because she's a very sought after substitute."

"I can see why she would be. The kids seem to respond to her."

"Well, she's been teaching for years. She probably knows all the tricks."

Denny grinned. "Yes, she does. I cornered her before the last bell and she shared some of them with me."

Mrs. Sheldon nodded. "I've noticed that the level of noise coming out of your room has gone down a few decibels, Mr. McCain."

Denny blushed. "You noticed?"

With a good-natured chuckle, Mrs. Sheldon said, "That's my job!"

"Have you heard from Miss Cook?" Denny asked, trying not to look too anxious.

"No, and what she's doing is highly unethical. You'd think she'd have the consideration to call me so that I'd have time to find a substitute for her room. I even checked on her mother, but she's not showing up for work either."

Denny remembered seeing Julia driving past him when he and Roscoe were out for a walk.

"Mrs. Sheldon, did you ever consider that maybe Julia's in trouble?"

"Oh, I doubt that very much. But maybe, since her mother is gone, too, there's some kind of family trouble? Do you think?"

Denny shrugged. "I guess we won't know until she comes back and tells us all about it." He picked up his briefcase, nodded to his principal, and walked out to his car. He could feel Mrs. Sheldon's eyes following him. What if his car didn't start? Since his dad hadn't come home last night, he'd have to call a tow truck.

That would *really* be embarrassing.

* * * *

Julia woke to complete darkness and silence. Panic had come and gone so many times, she didn't even try to struggle against her restraints. Her wrists were probably rubbed raw, but since they were tied behind her back, she had no way of checking. Squirming, she managed to move to a dry spot on the dirty floor after her bladder had emptied itself. Wasn't anyone going to check on her? At least someone should give her a drink of water. Right now, she'd be glad to see anyone, even the blue-eyed-pretend-cop. Weren't they missing her at school? The hours she had spent crying over the loss of her mother had exhausted her. She could now think about her in the past tense and not shed a tear.

In desperation, she gave a half-hearted jerk on her bound hands, closed her eyes, and willed herself to sleep.

CHAPTER 18

Night came quickly to the heavily wooded crash site. There was no time to search the area for water to clean his bloody head, but she examined it and found a deep cut on an egg-sized bump. The bleeding was no longer a problem. The new problem was that Charles was still insisting that he was Ryan Wilcox, the professional golfer. Along with the change of his name, there was a change in his personality. Charles the gentleman had turned into Ryan the playboy.

As the day rapidly turned into night, he was still looking around for his buddies whom he suspected were pulling a joke on him that wasn't funny anymore. When she called him Charles, the look of puzzlement on his face was real; he had no memory of the man named Charles. Susan finally convinced him that she wasn't an elderly groupie, but he tried once more at bedtime. When the coat was laid on a pile of gathered leaves and they were trying to figure out how to lie on one part and still have enough to throw over their bodies for cover, he looked at her wistfully. "Are you sure you aren't a groupie?"

The fur coat made a wonderful sleeping bag...for one person. There wasn't much wriggle room in the sleeping arrangement; the coat was huge, but so was he.

He had no problem falling asleep; Susan wasn't so fortunate. In order to stay covered by the coat, the two of them had fitted their bodies together. Susan's shorter frame was covered by the coat, but his legs were too long. He solved the problem by lying on his side, drawing up his knees until he fit inside the coat, and then pulling her close. The warmth coming from his body awakened emotions she hadn't felt since the long-ago days of her marriage. But, when in his sleep, he pulled her close and nuzzled her neck, she would have found it more acceptable if it had been Charles who was doing the nuzzling, but it wasn't Charles. It was Ryan.

Morning came with a mist falling out of a black sky. Inside their fur bed, the heat generated by their two bodies was very sensual. His reaction to waking up with his arms around a woman was instant, but not as instant as Susan's. Throwing off the coat, she jumped to her feet.

Shocked by the cold air, Susan gasped. It was Ryan who slowly opened his eyes and grinned up at her. "Hey, Babe, what are you doing out there in the cold? We have some unfinished business to take care of."

Susan rubbed the goosebumps on her arms. "There is no unfinished business!" she stated firmly.

Stretching out his long body, he bunched the coat around him and closed his eyes. "Well, then I guess you'll have to find some other way to keep warm."

The morning mist had turned into a drizzle. Desperate for shelter, Susan looked around and, except for the pile of wreckage that had been their plane, saw only trees. A snicker came from the pile of fur; Ryan had pulled the coat over his head.

"It's nice and dry in here...and it's warm, too. I'll bet you're *really* cold, aren't you? Come on, Suzie, crawl in. I'll warm you up!"

Susan pulled the collar of the blue sweatsuit jacket close to her neck. Just thinking how cold she would be right now in her short red dress made her shiver. She needed the warmth of the coat.

"Charles, I'll…"

Poking his head out of his fur cave, he interrupted, "Call me Ryan or I'm not listening".

"Okay. Ryan, please turn your back to me and I'll crawl in."

There was a moment of silence, followed by a rustling sound.

"Chicken."

Susan groaned. "I heard that!"

"Good. I meant for you to hear it."

The warmth that greeted her was seductive. Shivering, she longed to cuddle up to his warm body. She could feel him just inches away waiting to see what she was going to do.

"Ryan," she said quietly, "do you realize how much trouble we're in?"

Moving toward her, he whispered. "Trust me, Babe. You and me could get into some really hot trouble."

"Stop it!" she yelled. "We need to talk."

Ryan jerked away. "Jesus. You sound just like my wife."

Susan stiffened. "Your wife? Now you want to talk about your wife? The last time I mentioned the word, you shut down."

He looked puzzled. "You never asked me about my wife."

"Well, Charles told me he wasn't married."

"There you go with that Charles thing again!"

"Well, are you married? What about your wife?"

"I don't want to talk about her."

"You brought her up, I didn't."

He got very still. "Her name is Laura, and she, uh…." Finally, with a frown on his face, he turned to her. "I vaguely remember something about my wife and my caddy…I think it's important, but I can't remember what it is. I…I…really don't think I'm married any more."

"You did hit your head, you know."

Ryan reached up and touched the lump. "Wow! I sure did!"

Susan opened her mouth to say something but Ryan's hand shot out and covered her mouth.

"Listen!" he whispered.

Susan's eyes widened. She heard voices. Were they going to be rescued? The men's voices coming from the area of the wrecked plane were faint at first, but as they came nearer, words could be heard. Ryan kept shaking his head while clamping his hand over her mouth.

"They've got to be dead," declared a rough voice. "That plane is burned to a crisp."

"But what if they weren't? What if they're the feds and they're still alive? Answer me that!"

"Then we're in trouble!"

"What are you thinking?"

"I'm thinking just the two of us can't cover very much ground. We'll report that we've found the burned plane and then bring the rest of the workers back to search for dead bodies."

"And if we find them alive?"

"Then we'll turn them into dead bodies!"

The laughter that followed sent chills down Susan's spine. Ryan kept his hand over her mouth until silence once more reigned in the forest.

"Who were those awful men?" Susan whispered.

"I don't know, but whoever they are, they're willing to kill to keep this place a secret."

"So, whatever it is, the secret is right here where we crashed?"

"Seems so."

Ryan threw back the coat and stood up. "We've gotta move fast! Grab your stuff."

The stuff was the fur coat; everything else had burned up with the plane. Susan carried the heavy coat and Ryan was carrying nothing when he broke into a trot. He was far ahead of her when the sound of an airplane stopped both of them. Looking back over his shoulder, he was puzzled to see Susan frantically motioning him to do something…but what? Run? Hide? Climb a tree?

CHAPTER 19

Denny had a bad feeling in the pit of his stomach when he didn't spot the red convertible in the school's parking lot. How many days had it been since Julia and her mother had disappeared? The real estate office where Julia's mother worked had been no help. All the secretary knew was that Susan had had an appointment to show a vacant house to a transferee from Pittsburgh. She had picked up the key from Allen Real Estate before the showing, and then she had returned the key. That was the last anyone had seen her.

Before Mrs. McGregor had shared a few teaching techniques with him, his unruly class of eighth graders had worn him out. By the end of the school day, all he could think about was the comfortable couch waiting for him at home. Maybe it was Mrs. McGregor's help, or maybe he was just getting used to his job, but now after his classroom emptied, he no longer was thinking about the couch; he was thinking about Julia and her mother.

Picking up the phone book, he looked up the address of Susan Cook. If it had been a family problem that had called them away, chances were that both Susan and Julia would be together.

Denny drove slowly through the residential area of nicely landscaped lawns, and when he found the address that matched the one in the book, he pulled into the driveway and just sat there. Why was he here? Who was he to be nosing around in a co-workers business? But Denny couldn't shake the feeling that he needed to do something. He shrugged, opened the door, and stepped out.

The house looked empty. He had no idea what he had hoped to accomplish by visiting her mother's house. Not knowing what else to do, he was about to crawl back into his car when a man stepped out of the house next door and waved to him. *Susan has friendly neighbors*, he thought as he waved back.

When the man kept walking toward him, Denny realized that he had misread the wave; the man wasn't just being friendly. He wanted to talk.

With a hand held out in greeting, the man called, "I might just be a nosy neighbor, but are you looking for Susan Cook?"

Denny shook the offered hand. "I'm Denny McCain, and I teach school with her daughter, Julia. I *am* looking for Susan, because I'm thinking Julia might be with her mother."

The man dropped his hand. "Are you saying that Julia is missing?"

Denny nodded. "She hasn't shown up to teach her eighth grade class for two days."

"Oh," the man muttered. "That's not good!"

"Wh...wh...what do you mean by that?" Denny demanded.

"I'm Joe Binder. My wife and I have lived beside Susan for years. We've watched Julia grow up. Great kid! Shame she's missing."

"I don't know her very well, Mr. Binder. I just met her the other day when I subbed at her school. But I didn't peg her as being an irresponsible person who would just take off without calling her principal."

"No, you're right. The Julia I know would never do something like that. Come with me. I want to show you something."

Denny followed the man into Susan's yard. Joe didn't say a thing when he stopped in front of the big picture window; he just pointed.

Denny gasped. "That's a bullet hole?"

"Yes, and I'm afraid it's not the only one."

Denny was afraid of the answer to his next question. "When did this happen?"

Joe shook his head. "I really don't know. My wife and I were gone for a few days, and when we got home, there was a cop car in Susan's driveway. Of course, we asked him what was going on, and he said not to worry, that he had taken care of everything, and the police were on the case. What case? I asked him. He told me to mind my own business and let the police do their job."

Denny snorted. "Our tax dollars pay his salary."

"After he left, my wife and I came over here and found the bullet hole in the window, and if you look closely, you'll find bullet holes in the side of the house. That's when we called the local station and talked to Officer Allen. You can imagine how surprised we were when he didn't know what we were talking about. He and Detective Hatch spent a long time in that house, but if they found anything, they didn't tell us."

"Are you thinking that the cop you talked to wasn't really a cop... or a dirty cop?"

Joe nodded.

"What did the cop look like?"

"He was young and rather good looking. It was his blue eyes that I remember. Have you ever seen a picture of the sled dogs in Alaska?"

Denny nodded.

"Well, that's the color of his eyes. If you ever see a man in a policeman's uniform who has eyes like that, you'll know he's the dirty cop."

Joe was still standing on Susan's driveway when Denny backed out and headed for home. He had picked up some useful information from Joe, but what could he do with it? He was convinced that both mother and daughter were in trouble, and judging by the bullet holes in Susan's house, they were in serious trouble.

While he was waiting for the light to change, the tantalizing smell of grilled hamburgers and onions reminded him that he'd missed dinner. Since the smell was coming from a fast-food restaurant on the corner, he swung his car into the parking lot. The thought of taking the food home and eating by himself didn't seem appealing, so he parked and went inside. At least there would be people around him while he ate.

It was when he was carrying his tray while looking for an empty table that he saw the blue-eyed policeman dumping his tray and heading for the door. Without a moment's hesitation, Denny grabbed his own wrapped sandwich off the tray and ran after him. By the time he reached his old junker, he could see the taillights of the police car disappearing into the stream of traffic. Denny held his breath and didn't let it out until the engine turned over.

All Denny knew about following someone was what he had picked up watching cop shows on television. But in all those chases he'd watched, not one of the cars doing the chasing had ever been a beat-up-hard-to-miss-wreck-of-a-car like his. He had to hang so far back that he was a block and a half behind the police car when he saw it pulling into a driveway. Denny swung into a side street and parked.

Not wanting to be seen by the blue-eyed cop, Denny's progress was serenaded by barking dogs as he ran through private backyards. Panting, he stopped at the house before the one with the police car in the driveway. He had no idea what he was going to find by following the blue-eyed cop, or what he would say to him if he did confront him. He was about to turn around when the sound of a familiar voice stopped him cold. It was his dad's voice.

There was a thick over-grown hedge that hadn't seen a clipper in years which gave Denny cover as he crawled closer to the two men. His dad was using his temper, trying to make the blue-eyed cop do something. Denny recognized what he was doing because his dad used that technique on him all the time. It didn't seem to be working on the cop, though.

"No!" the cop was shaking his head. "I didn't sign up to kill anyone!"

"Come on now. Why do you want to wreck all the good points you racked up by grabbing the girl's cell phone?"

"Don't call her 'the girl'! Her name is Julia!" Denny could hear emotion in the cop's voice.

"Ah, I see. You're a little sweet on her, aren't you? And how much do you think that will help you? The police would love to hear her describe your blue eyes."

The cop hung his head. "Can't someone else do it...please?"

Denny couldn't hear what his dad was saying but he could see his fingers poking the cop's chest repeatedly as the cop tried to back away. The scared look on the cop's face didn't leave even when Denny saw his dad's car drive away.

What was the cop going to do now? Was Julia inside the house? Had his dad talked the man into killing her? Denny watched him put his hands over his face as he muttered something as if he were praying. With a deep sigh, the cop turned and walked into the house.

Denny's head was in a whirl. He had no weapon but he just couldn't stay out here and pray that nothing would happen. All that he had going for him was the one thing that had bugged him all his adult life; he and his dad looked and sounded alike. What had his dad been wearing? It was hard to think clearly when he was so scared but he finally remembered that his dad had on a white shirt and a black pair of pants. If Denny took off his jacket, then he and his father would be dressed alike. Denny glanced down at his pants. They were a dark navy blue, the kind that, if you don't pay attention, can be taken as black.

Armed with nothing, Denny approached the front door and entered the house. A terrible smell of vomit hit him immediately. Trying to stifle his own gag reflex, he walked into the room with his arm over his nose; he almost bumped into the blue-eyed cop who had stopped at the threshold of a room.

Denny couldn't see what had made Blue Eyes gag, but he did recognize the chewed-up Big Mac in the vomit the cop's s stomach had deposited on the floor.

Spinning around, the man's first response when he saw Denny was one of abject terror.

Utter panic was replaced with unbelievable release when Robert heard Mr. McCain say, "Get out of here! I'll take care of this myself."

"Mr. McCain!"

Denny reeled back from the cop's sour breath.

"Thank God you came back! Oh, thank you, thank you!" the man cried as he ran out of the house. Denny heard the police car's squealing tires as it backed out of the driveway.

Denny slowly entered the foul-smelling room. A small crumpled body lay curled up in a corner. Could that be Julia? If it was, was she still alive?

Picking his way across the room, trying not to step into the puddle of urine and vomit, he knelt down beside the body.

Julia felt a presence. No one had checked on her since the day she'd overheard the blue-eyed cop and his partner arguing over who was going to kill her. Had the argument been settled? Knowing that she was too weak to fight back, she closed her eyes and waited for the first blow.

In order to see the face, Denny rolled the unmoving figure.

"Julia! Open your eyes!"

Julia jerked.

"Julia, it's Denny! Please open your eyes!"

Denny had found her! But could she trust him?

"I've got to get you out of here before anyone else shows up!"

The urgency in his voice settled the question.

Her eyelids raised, and in a faint voice she murmured, "What took you so long?" Her eyelids closed, only to fly open when she felt Denny's arms around her.

In a weak voice, she protested, "Denny, I'm a mess! Please don't pick me up! I...I'm embarrassed."

"Hush! We need to get out of here!"

"But I'm...I'm not clean! Please."

Denny's arms tightened around her.

" Wait! Maybe I could walk and then you wouldn't have to carry me."

Denny almost grinned. "It's kinda hard to walk when your feet are tied together. Just hold on and with any luck we'll be out of here before anyone comes to check on you."

Denny was in shock. What kind of animals had done this to Julia? He felt nothing but disgust when he realized that his dad was one of the animals.

Gathering Julia in his arms, he staggered out of the room. He needed to find a place to put her while he ran back for his car. Looking around, he decided that the hedge he had hidden behind to eavesdrop on his dad and Old Blue Eyes would work. While wrapping his discarded jacket around her, he whispered into her ear, "I'll be right back."

Minutes later, Julia, with her restraints removed, was lying on the back seat of his old junker, and he was behind the wheel driving...to where? He didn't have a clue.

With no destination in mind, Denny drove aimlessly. There were no stirrings or sounds coming from the backseat. How many days had she gone without water? The hospital would be the logical place to take her, but if dirty police were really involved in this mess, taking her to where they would have access to her would be a big mistake. Oh, if only he had a place of his own. But, he didn't, and nothing could be done about that now. He shuddered when he thought how awful it would have been had he not known that his dad was involved. Right now he'd be headed home with Julia to ask his dad to help him take care of her. He was finding out things about his dad that were making him uncomfortable. Their relationship had never been good but he'd never thought of his dad as being cruel. At the next light, he turned around and studied the quiet girl lying on his back seat. There was no doubt in his mind; his dad was responsible for this and he was evil.

Horns blaring behind him jarred him back to reality; the light was green.

It was as if the car knew where to go. When his aimless driving took him past Susan's house, the steering wheel just seemed to take over. The next thing Denny knew, he had driven into Joe Binder's driveway.

With his head resting on the steering wheel, Denny sat in his car and prayed. He looked at Julia once more through the rearview mirror. "Am I doing the right thing?" he asked her prone form. When she didn't answer him, Denny put the car in park and turned it off.

He sighed, opened the car door, and got out. If the Binders turned Julia away, then what? He thought he'd heard real affection in Joe's voice when he talked about Julia, but did that give Denny the right to ask them to risk their lives? Harboring Julia could be very dangerous.

Mrs. Binder answered his knock on the door. "Whatever you're selling, young man, I'm not buying."

The door was almost closed before Denny was able to cry, "No, no, don't close the door. Is Mr. Binder in?"

"He's not buying anything, either!"

A voice from inside asked, "Who's at the door, hon?"

"Just a kid driving an old junker car. Probably wants a hand-out."

Denny breathed a sigh of relief. "Mr. Binder?" he yelled. "You remember me? Julia and I teach at the same school."

Joe pushed his wife aside. "I sure do! Are you here with news? Have Julia and her mother been found?"

"I don't know anything about her mother, but I found Julia. She's in bad shape but I'm afraid to take her to the hospital. She's on the back seat of my *old junker* car."

Mrs. Binder winced apologetically.

"Why did you bring her here?" Joe asked.

Denny shrugged. "Where else can I take her?"

Mrs. Binder pushed her husband out of the way. "You say someone hurt little Julia?"

"It's mostly that she's been tied up and ignored for two days, but they intended to do more than hurt her, Mrs. Binder."

"Oh my!" Mrs. Binder cried. "I'll bet that blue-eyed cop has something to do with this!"

"There are others, but yes, the cop had a lot to do with this. He was ordered to kill Julia."

"K...k...kill her?" stammered Mrs. Binder.

"Those were his orders." Denny winced just remembering his own father's voice giving the order.

"And all of this is tied to what happened next door?"

"Possibly, but I have no idea what's going on. I just know Julia is in danger. Will you help?"

The Binders didn't say anything; they just looked into each other's eyes. Their silent communication ended when Mrs. Binder's head nodded slightly.

Joe turned to Denny. "We want to help. How badly is she hurt?"

"She's probably very hungry, but her main problem is dehydration. For at least two days, they kept her tied up in a closed room. She needs to be cleaned, Mrs. Binder."

"I'm not a nurse, but I'm willing to try. And would you please quit calling me Mrs. Binder? Judy is my name."

"Okay, Judy it is."

"Bring her in."

Denny heaved a big sigh of relief.

CHAPTER 20

By the time the plane was directly overhead, Ryan had figured out that Susan was concerned that someone in the plane might be looking for them. But wasn't that what they wanted? When he saw Susan crouch close to a tree trunk with the dark brown fur coat over her, he got the message. To anyone searching from above, she blended into the bark on the trees. Ryan shrugged and went along with her. Grabbing a low branch, he climbed a tree and didn't jump down until the plane was gone.

With his arms crossed and his foot tapping, he waited for Susan to catch up with him.

"Wanna tell me what that camouflage bit was about?"

Susan shook her head. "Not now! We have to get far away from the crash site before we can do anything! Let's go!"

"I'm not moving until you promise."

Looking back over her shoulder she yelled, "Well, when they catch you, tell them I said Hi!"

Susan didn't get too far into the deep woods before he caught up with her. The trees gave them some protection from the rain, but without being able to see the sun's journey across the sky, they had no idea in what direction they were running.

After a half hour run, Susan grabbed her side and bent over.

"Problem?" Ryan stopped running and went back to her.

"Got a stitch in my side," panted Susan.

"It's time for a rest," he agreed. "I'm going to climb a tree and look around for a water supply. We can go for days without food, but we won't last long without water."

Finding a big log, Susan sat down, draped the coat over her head, and shivered into its warmth. The man she knew as Charles had given her the coat, and now as Ryan, he was so familiar with it that he didn't even question how she had come to possess it. At what point in his life had Ryan become Charles? Whenever it was, Ryan wasn't remembering any of it.

From the top of the tree, Ryan called down. "I have good news, and I have bad news."

Susan peeked out of her fur cover. "Let's do the good news first."

"Okay. The good news is there's a stream of water quite close to where we are."

"Great! I'm really thirsty. Can we go there now?"

"Don't you want to hear the bad news?"

"Do I really have to?"

"I think you do."

"Couldn't I hear it after I get a drink?"

"Susan, behave! The bad news is the burned-out plane is between us and the stream."

"Burned-out plane?" The coat slid to the ground as she jumped to her feet. "Are you telling me that we've walked in a circle?"

"Uh, it was more like we *ran* in a circle!"

"Oh, for God's sake!" she cried. "We're right back where we started?"

Ryan slid down from the tree. "Afraid so."

Susan bent down, picked up the coat, and brushed it off. "You know, maybe it's not so bad that we ended up back here. This area would have been the first place they searched. What are the chances that they'd check it out it again?"

Ryan thought for a moment. "That's a good point. I suppose we'll be as safe around here as anywhere else. Let's go inspect the stream, and while we're cleaning up, I'll tell you about what I found in the tree."

Susan nodded. "I have some things I have to tell you, too."

"Dare I hope that one of things is the reason you didn't want to be spotted by someone in the plane?"

* * * *

Ryan looked up from lapping water like a dog to watch Susan's sorry attempt to use her hands as a cup.

"Give it up, Suzie! You'll die of thirst before you'll get a drink that way."

Susan threw the coat aside, stretched out on the ground, and stuck her face into the water…and quickly jerked it back out.

"Hey, I just saw a fish!"

"Really? Do you have any idea how we could catch it?"

"No, I don't, but we'd better figure out how to catch something real soon or we're going to get really hungry."

"Oh, this is good!" Ryan sputtered between laps.

"Yes, it sure is, but now my stomach's growling! I didn't care for the meal you made this morning before we took off in the plane. Whoever heard of beans and corn for breakfast? But right now just thinking about it makes my mouth water."

Ryan quit drying his face on his jacket sleeve. "Wait a minute! You say I made breakfast for you?"

"If you call canned corn and canned beans breakfast, then yes," she said sourly.

The puzzled look on his face was replaced by a sly grin. "Does that mean we spent the night together and I don't remember it?"

Before Susan had a chance to answer, the sound of men's voices in the distance brought both of them to their feet.

Ryan whispered, "Remember that I said I had something to show you? I was going to surprise you with my discovery later, but we need it now! We have to go back to the tree that I climbed. Now run!"

Susan grabbed the coat and ran.

Panting, she stood at the base of a tree, frantically looking around for Ryan. No matter how hard she'd tried to keep up with him, his long legs and the heavy coat had put an uncomfortable distance between them. At the end, she'd just run, hoping it was in the right direction.

Out of breath, she stopped under what looked like the right tree, but then so did a lot of others. How could he do this to her? Leaving her alone like this, surrounded by men who, in their own words, wanted to make her into a dead body? She was working her way toward a full panic attack when she heard a voice coming from the top of the tree.

"Well, are you going to stand down there all day?"

Looking up, Susan saw him sitting on a branch looking pleased with himself.

"Well, I'm here, but no thanks to you! How could you leave me like that? Charles would never have deserted me the way you did!"

"There we go with the Charles thing again!" Ryan sounded peeved. "I thought you'd given up on that."

"No, I haven't given up. I was just waiting for the right time to talk about him," Susan snapped, "like now."

"But not before I get to show you what I've found up here."

"You found something in the tree?"

"Yes. Hold on, I'm coming down."

Susan watched Ryan scamper down the tree until he stopped at the lowest branch. "Throw the coat to me, then give me your hand. The first step is the hardest. After that, the branches are like steps that go up to almost the top of the tree."

Susan had never been much of a tree-climber, but Ryan was right; the branches were like steps. In a short period of time, Susan found herself higher in the tree than she liked.

"Don't look down," cautioned Ryan. "Now just one more step up and then to the right," he pointed at another good handhold. "Here you go."

Susan found herself standing on what looked like a platform. "What is this?"

"A treehouse. Why would someone build a treehouse in the middle of the forest?"

"Have you found anything else?" she asked.

"Like what?"

"Like the garbage bag that's wedged in a crevice on the other side of the trunk."

"Oh, I didn't see that!" Ryan exclaimed. Reaching around the trunk, he retrieved the bag.

"Are we going to open it?" whispered Susan.

"It's probably nothing but someone's garbage, but why are you whispering?" Ryan whispered back.

"I don't know…maybe the one who owns the bag is nearby?"

"Finders keepers, losers weepers," Ryan chanted as he opened the bag.

What was in the bag was worth more than silver or gold. They couldn't believe that they were actually looking at a jar of peanut butter, a box of crackers, four apples, and four candy bars along with a knife and a plastic cup. The bottom of the bag held a blanket and clothes that looked clean, a toothbrush and toothpaste, a mirror, a flashlight, a telescope, and one thick book.

The two of them stared at the bag's contents.

"What in the world…?" wondered Susan.

"I think we've stumbled onto someone who, for some reason, wants to watch, but doesn't want to be seen. Either that, or he's a lookout to spot approaching trouble."

Ryan picked up the book and rifled through its pages.

"You have a surprised look on your face," Susan observed.

"Well, since I was expecting the book to be a novel, I'm surprised because it's not. It's a medical book. From the well-worn pages, I'd say this book is owned by a medical student."

With her eyebrows raised, Susan asked, "A medical student living in a treehouse?"

Ryan shrugged and closed the book.

Susan looked with longing at the food. "Dare we eat it?"

Grinning, Ryan unwrapped a candy bar and waved it under her nose. "Watch!"

Being practical, Susan divided the apples and candy bars. "Now, don't eat it all at once! This might be the only food we'll see in a long time."

"Yes, Mother," Ryan mocked.

"Suit yourself, but you aren't getting any of mine after your supply runs out!"

After each had eaten half of the candy bar Ryan had unwrapped and half an apple, Susan spread out the fur coat and motioned for Ryan to sit by her. "Ready for a story?" she asked.

Ryan sat down and folded his long legs under him. "Is this story about this Charles fellow who you think I am?"

Susan nodded. "It all started one day when I was at work at the real estate office …yes, I'm a realtor…when a call came in from a man who introduced himself as Charles Holiday, an unmarried man from Pittsburgh. He said he was transferring into my area, and asked if I could find a house for him. After that, every few weeks he'd call and say he was back in town, and I'd show him anything that had come on the market since his last visit. Monday, I showed him one house…." Susan paused. "Oh, so much has happened, it's hard to believe that it was just three days ago!"

Ryan sat at the edge of his seat listening intently. When she described the scene where she'd dropped the house key and ended up landing on her backside, Ryan threw his head back and laughed.

"That's exactly what Charles did," Susan grinned.

"After coffee, we split. I went home, and since Charles was a transferee, I pictured him at a motel."

"So far, so good. I'm a bit bored, though. When does the story get interesting?"

"Right about now. I was at home minding my own business...."

Ryan was hanging onto her every word. ". ...and that's when bullets started hitting the house and coming through the windows."

"And then what happened?"

Susan continued, describing the flight out her back door, the crawl through her yard to the garage, the encounter with the skunk, and ended the story with the plane crash that had turned Charles into Ryan.

Ryan hadn't moved a muscle. Susan had watched as different expressions flashed across his face as he listened to the story. Had any of it sounded familiar to him?

"And did this Charles tell you why he was running?"

"No, he didn't."

With a sharp intake of breath, Ryan exclaimed, "I do remember that my wife was acting funny, but she wouldn't tell me what was bothering her!"

Susan watched as a far-away look appeared in Ryan's eye.

Shaking his head and focusing his eyes on Susan, he said, "Move over. That's my coat you're sitting on. How did you get it?"

"Charles gave it to me. He said a famous golfer gave it to him as a joke."

"Yeah," Ryan grinned. "I hate to play golf when it's cold, and one year it snowed halfway through a game. I complained...a lot"

"That's exactly what Charles said."

"Hmmm," Ryan murmured.

"And what do you remember of those years?"

"They seem to be there...I know that they're there... but everything's hazy. Nothing sticks out that make me remember anything special. Oh yes, I do remember my best friend, Ted. He was not only my caddy, he was also my favorite cousin. We looked so much alike, people got us mixed up....." Ryan paused as if remembering Ted was important. "And then one day I woke up beside a burning plane, and you were yelling at Charles to open his eyes."

Susan reached over and felt the large swollen lump on his head. "So, you've lost a lot of memory of the years before the crash. Don't you wonder how much time there is between Ryan and Charles? You didn't recognize my cell phone, and they've been around for some time. I would imagine that your appearance has changed over the years, too."

"I hadn't thought about it, but you're right. Wasn't there a mirror in the bag?"

Susan rummaged through the bag and pulled out the mirror. "Have a look at yourself, Ryan."

The startled shout coming out of Ryan's mouth alarmed her.

"What the hell?" he cried.

"Ryan, what's wrong?"

"This is not my face! I've never seen this man before!"

CHAPTER 21

Dennis McCain drove by the house he'd been watching for almost two years. Allen Real Estate presently listed the house, but during those years he'd lost count of the number of times the owner, desperate to sell, had switched real estate companies. Today there was a foreclosure notice on the house; the bank now owned it.

Acting as if he were the owner of the house, the for-rent ads that he'd placed in out-of-area papers brought him three potential suckers. He didn't expect to score on all three, but the odds were good that at least one of them would return the signed rental form along with a check for the first and last month's rent. The scammed renter might even arrive in town and be moved into the house before the fraud was discovered. "Caveat Emptor," Dennis muttered under his breath.

Finding the foreclosure sign was good, but Dennis had something else on his mind. Earlier today when he'd dropped into the rental house they'd been using, he found Robert on his hands and knees cleaning the room that had been Julia's cell. Since Robert had been so reluctant to kill Julia, Dennis had expected to see a disturbed and troubled man. Instead, Robert had greeted him with such enthusiasm that Dennis had to do some fancy footwork to dodge a hug. Dennis also found it strange that Robert kept thanking him. For what? Had he taken advantage of the situation and had a bit of fun with Julia before he did away with her? Dennis really didn't care.

Looking at his watch, he noted that Denny would be home from school by now, probably cooking dinner for the two of them. His son wouldn't dare ask him why he hadn't come home last night.

* * * *

It was the end of the school day and there wasn't a student to be seen or heard in the quiet hall as Denny made his way to the exit. He was hoping to sneak out unnoticed; he really didn't want to answer questions about Julia. With his hand on the doorknob, Denny thought he had managed to slip by Mrs. Sheldon when he heard, "Mr. McCain, please step into my office."

The feeling in the pit of Denny's stomach was familiar. As a mischievous student, he had heard those words more times than he even wanted to think about. But he no longer was a student; he was a substitute teacher who wanted to keep the job even if it were only for a few weeks. Had he done something wrong? Maybe she wanted to congratulate him for the progress he had made in controlling his class. It surprised him that his voice was actually shaking when he asked, "You wanted to see me?"

"Yes. I was wondering if you'd heard anything from Miss Cook. This was the third day that I've had to scramble around to get a substitute for her class."

Denny took a deep breath; he wasn't in trouble but Julia was. His arms twitched remembering how they'd felt when they carried Julia to safety last night. "Oh, uh... are you saying she still hasn't called you?"

"No, she hasn't, and I'm starting to worry. The real estate company that her mother works for is getting concerned, too. Her employer wouldn't say too much, but they have the local police looking into the matter."

Denny's head jerked. "The local police?" Was she talking about Old Blue Eyes?

"Yes, he mentioned Officer Tom Allen."

Denny was thinking fast. "I don't know Officer Allen. Is he the one with eyes like an Alaskan husky?"

Mrs. Sheldon laughed. "Now that's a funny way to describe blue eyes, but no, Officer Allen has green eyes and red hair. He drops in once in a while to talk to the children about good bicycle safety habits."

Denny relaxed.

"But," Mrs. Sheldon continued, "if her unexcused absence goes on much longer, I'm afraid Miss Cook will have to look for employment somewhere other than this school district."

"I don't know Miss Cook that well, but she didn't strike me as being an irresponsible person." Denny took a deep breath, and even though he knew that Susan Cook was probably dead, he added, "I'd hate to think that she's in trouble, but the fact that her mother is also missing is disturbing."

"Well," Mrs. Sheldon said in dismissing him, "let me know if you hear anything."

Denny left the school and walked slowly to his car. Tonight, when his dad walked in the door expecting to have his dinner on the table, how was he going to look at him? He had no idea what his dad was into, but he had heard with his own ears his dad order Blue Eyes to kill Julia. He didn't even want to think of the nice couple he'd put in danger by showing up at their door with Julia.

* * * *

Julia, dressed in Judy's sweatsuit, sat shivering by the fireplace. The events of the past three days had taken their toll. On the outside she looked calm, but on the inside she was falling apart. Her nerves were stretched, she jumped at every little noise, and she couldn't get warm. The bandages on her wrists covered skin that had been rubbed raw by the bindings she had struggled against.

And her mother. How could she be dead? But she had heard the blue-eyed cop say they had traced the cell phone call her mother had made to her. The thought that the call to her might have been the cause of her mother's death was shattering.

And her teaching job; what was Mrs. Sheldon thinking about her now? Would she even have a job after this was all over? Her mind went to Denny. If he hadn't intervened, she'd be dead by now. She'd heard him tell the Binders that he couldn't risk coming back to check on her. According to him, it was just a matter of time before his dad figured out what had happened. Then Denny would be in deep trouble.

The Binders were so sweet. How much danger was she bringing to these nice people? Mrs. Binder had been like a second mother to her. On report card day, she had always stopped at the Binders' house before she went home. The fact that Mrs. Binder gave her a cookie for every 'A' had something to do with it, but that wasn't the whole reason. A child knows what real affection feels like and Julia had felt it when she was at the Binders.

CHAPTER 22

"This is not my face! I've never seen this man before!"

An unexpected voice agreed. "That makes two of us but I'm gonna shoot you anyway!"

Ryan and Susan whirled around, shocked to see a young girl, probably in her early teens, pointing a gun at them. The long blond hair that hung down and partially covered her face gave her a tough gangster-like look.

Susan screamed.

"Shut your mouth, lady!"

"Please don't shoot us!" Susan pleaded. "We mean you no harm!"

Seeing the open bag, the girl snarled, "No harm? You're sitting in my home, eating my food, and you say you mean me no harm? Now you're really gonna die!"

Her home? The treehouse was her home? The girl, dressed in men's clothes that, while clean, were several sizes too large for her. Trying to sound tough, she was using both hands to hold the gun that Ryan easily recognized; it was a toy.

Breathing a relieved sigh, he cried, "Thank God you found us!"

"W...w...what?"

"Didn't you see the burned plane?"

The gun wavered.

"Y...y...you were in the plane and you didn't die?"

"We got out before the plane exploded. Now would you please put down the gun?"

With a calmed sigh, she lowered the gun. "So that's who you are!"

"Yes, that's who we are. We just needed a place to hide from the men who were ordered to kill any survivors."

"They aren't looking anymore. They're sure that whoever was in the plane burned up with it."

The knot of fear in his stomach receded a bit. "That's good to know! But who are they, and why do they want to kill us? We heard them talking."

"They probably think you're the feds."

Ryan raised his eyebrows. "What if we were?"

"Well, are you?"

"No, no, I mean, why are they afraid of the feds? What's going on?"

"What's going on?" The girl sounded disgusted. "They're growing *things*...if you know what I mean."

"They? Who is growing things? Your family?" Ryan asked.

The girl snorted. "Those bullies... my family? I don't think so!"

Susan's motherly instincts kicked in. "You said this was your home. Why are you out here all alone?"

She shrugged. "It just happened."

"No, no!" Susan disagreed. "A girl doesn't live in a tree because it 'just happened'. Who feeds you? Who clothes you?"

"My dad, of course!"

Susan's eyebrows shot up. "Your dad allows you to live in a tree? I've never heard of such a thi ...." Her mouth slammed shut; the gun that the girl was again pointing at her looked huge.

"I want you to know that my dad takes good care of me!" the girl cried. "I'd be dead if Dad hadn't built me the treehouse!"

Susan tried to ignore the gun that was still pointed at her. "Dead? The growers would kill you?"

The girl shuddered. "Eventually, they would. I don't even want to think what they would do to me before they killed me."

Susan gasped. "Oh, my!"

The gun waivered. "So, don't you *dare* say anything bad about my dad!"

"B…b…but he has a place to live, and you don't? Why aren't you with him?"

"He lives in the farm house with the growers. They don't know that I exist, and we've got to keep it that way."

Seeing the girl was getting upset, Ryan stepped in. "Could you please put the toy gun away and tell us what happened?"

"'Toy?" Susan questioned.

The girl hung her head. "You knew."

Ryan nodded.

Her face clouded. "Okay, so it's not real, but why should I tell you anything? I don't know if you're the good guys or the bad guys!"

Susan smiled her kindest smile. "Now, look at us. Do we really look like the bad guys?"

The girl shrugged. "I haven't talked to anyone other than my dad for more than a year."

Shocked, Susan repeated, "A year?"

"Yes, a year! And another winter is coming! I barely lived through the last one." The girl looked back and forth between the two strangers who had found her treehouse. "Are you really the good guys?"

Ryan shrugged. "I guess you'll have to take our word for it."

The girl's eyes narrowed as she tried to make up her mind. With a nod of her head, she finally said, "Oh, well, here's what happened. But I'm telling you right now, when you find a way out of here, you're taking me with you!"

After making the declaration, she leaned back against the tree. With one hand absentmindedly finger combing the knots out of her tangled hair, she closed her eyes and started talking. "It was going to be a big adventure, moving from the city to the farm," the girl paused and sighed. "Mom inherited the farm from her parents, but since Grandpa hadn't farmed the last few years of his life, it wasn't much of a working farm. Dad never wanted to be a farmer, and because this farm is so isolated, we never had any plans to move here. But things happened. First, Dad lost his job, the bank took our house, and then Mom got sick."

Opening her eyes, she brushed away a tear that was running down her face. "Mom died."

The three sat in silence for a moment.

She cleared her throat. "So, Dad and I packed up and came to the farm. When we got here, Dad was surprised to see that someone was living in the house. While he went to check it out, I ran after a little black and white kitten that I saw disappearing into the barn. I never did catch it, but when I looked back, I saw men with guns tying up my dad."

Susan gasped.

"I didn't know what to do! And then Dad managed to look my way. He mouthed the word 'run', and I did."

"So, they really don't know about you."

"Jeez lady, didn't I already tell you that?" the girl huffed. "I was terrified thinking they probably had killed my dad. What was going to happen to me? I found the stream, so I had water, and I found patches of berries, so I had something to eat. Nighttime was the worst. I had to sleep on the ground and just thinking about all the bugs and spiders that could crawl all over me...." The girl stopped, closed her eyes, and shuddered.

"Go on," urged Susan.

The girl opened her eyes. "Sorry," she grinned. "I just hate spiders!"

"Me, too!" Ryan chimed in. Rubbing his head, he looked puzzled. "I think I do."

"Sure, you do! Everyone hates spiders," Susan declared. "Now, continue with the story! I have to know what happened next."

"One night I was trying to convince myself that what was crawling up my leg wasn't a spider, when the sound of men's voices got me all excited. I thought it was my dad finally coming to find me."

"At this point, how many nights had it been?" Susan asked.

The girl shrugged. "I was so terrified I can't really say. Maybe five?"

Ryan frowned at Susan. "Quit interrupting the story!"

"Sorry about that. So, tell us about the men. I take it your dad wasn't one of them?"

"No, he wasn't. They were heading to right where I was, and I had nowhere to go. So I pulled myself up to a low branch of the nearest tree."

Susan nodded. "That was fast thinking!"

"In the morning, I climbed to the top to get a better idea of where I was. I could see the house and some fields growing plants that I didn't recognize. By this time, I was getting pretty tired of eating berries, but the thought of having to go to the house where I'd seen how rough the men had been when they took my dad...well, what were my options? I was about to panic ...and then Dad showed up. He'd talked them into letting him live because he convinced them they needed a cook; he claimed he was a good one."

"Is he?" asked Ryan.

She crinkled up her nose. "He had never cooked a thing until Mom died...then he got pretty clever with eggs."

"So, he lives in the house, and you live out here. Is he free to come and go as he wishes?" Susan asked.

The girl shrugged. "They put some kind of gadget on his leg that he can't get off. He can only go so far away from the house before it makes a loud noise."

"Then who brings you food and clothes?"

"My dad. He picked a tree that was in the direction of the dump where he goes with the garbage every evening. It's also an area of light foot traffic. There's really no reason for the workers to come to this part of the woods. He built me the treehouse, and he sneaks food and clothes to me."

"Don't the workers wonder where he goes? And where did he get the material to build your treehouse?"

"Dad was helping the workers build a shed to hold the crops before they are flown out. He took a few things, and when no one seemed to notice, he stole enough to make me this platform; there's another one higher up."

"How safe are you here?"

"I can't say the workers *never* come into this part of the woods, because they do. In order for them not to notice my tracks, Dad picked a tree that had a path real close by. When I leave the path, I always take different routes to my tree."

"The farm…do you have any neighbors? Couldn't you find someone to help you?"

The girl shook her head. "One reason we never wanted to move here is because the farm is so isolated. Maybe my grandparents were hermits, I don't know because I never saw very much of them, but why else would they want to live so far away from everyone and everything? Grandpa had learned to fly in the service so they moved here and built a landing strip. The road to get here is just an old rutted logging trail. It was easier for my grandparents to fly in and out instead driving on the trail. So you see, there's really no place I can go for help. Believe me, if there were, I'd have run there a long time ago."

Susan shook her head in incredulity. "This is hard to believe."

"I couldn't believe it myself for the longest time. If someone had told me that I'd be living in a treehouse in constant fear of being discovered…." Covering her face with her hands, she shuddered.

The three sat in silence waiting for the girl to continue. "When my grandparents left, I guess the growers thought they could get away with moving in."

"How big an operation is it?" Susan asked.

"The soil is good for what they're growing. They built a big greenhouse with all kinds of bright lights inside. You can see it at night if you climb the right tree."

"How do they get their product out of here?" Ryan wanted to know.

"They use the landing strip. I hear planes coming and going."

"Wait a minute!" Ryan cried. "Why don't they see you when they fly over your tree?"

"They very seldom fly in this direction. But just in case, Dad keeps me supplied with fresh branches to camouflage my platform."

Susan looked at Ryan. "Too bad you aren't Charles. He can fly a plane, and you can't."

Ryan gave her a dirty look. "You have to admit that Charles didn't handle his last flight very well."

The girl looked sharply at the two of them. "Can you get me out of here?"

Ryan shook his head. "We don't have any idea how to get ourselves out of here."

"But you have to! I don't know what month or what day it is, but I do know that I've spent a winter out here. Look at the leaves! They're turning color already." Covering her face with her hands, she shuddered. "I don't know if I can survive another one."

"What about school?" Susan asked.

"No one knows I'm here. You two are the first people I've talked to in all that time. Dad brings me books, makes assignments…but it's not like being in school." With a faraway look in her eyes, she added, "I'm missing the dances, the football games, friends…."

Susan looked at the girl who was wearing ill fitted men's clothing that hung off her shoulders more like a comfy robe than a shirt. Her blond hair was a tangled mess, and although she looked clean, there was an unkempt air about her. Susan was hit with an unexpected urge; she wanted to reach out and hug the girl. Instead, she asked, "Don't you think it's about time we introduce ourselves?"

CHAPTER 23

Dennis turned the drawer upside down and impatiently kicked at the socks and shorts as they tumbled to the floor. Since he hadn't smoked a cigarette in years, he had no idea why he thought he'd find an unfinished pack in with his underwear. Desperate times call for desperate measures.

Something was seriously wrong with Robert. It had gotten so bad Dennis planned his day around *not* running into the blue-eyed cop. To begin with, anyone with such distinctive physical features should never go astray of the law; victims would have no problem remembering those icy blue eyes. Dennis shuddered when he relived the moment when Robert had winked one of those eyes at him. Why was Robert winking at him? It was quite unnerving.

Robert wasn't the only reason for the frenzied cigarette search. Dennis hated it when one of his little rackets hit a snag, and one had. Who would have ever guessed that the last realtor to have the listing on the house before it had gone into foreclosure would get her hands on an out-of-area newspaper? He had no way of knowing that she'd been watching the house closely, hoping that when the bank put the foreclosed property back on the market they'd give the listing to her. When she alerted the bank that someone was advertising one of their foreclosed properties for rent, the scam was exposed. After the con had been brought to light, several couples had spoken out that they had been swindled in a similar deal but had been too embarrassed to report it.

As long as another one of his schemes kept filling his pockets, Dennis, as an investor of other people's money, could continue to live the good life. It constantly surprised him how easily he could talk people into parting with their money by offering them a high rate of return; old people were the easiest marks. Keeping good records and making phony investment statements was boring. For those reasons, he kept the operation small.

It was just for the money that Dennis had gotten involved in the contract to kill the professional golfer. The day he had help set fire to the man's house and barn he'd felt more compassion for the cars in the barn than he'd felt for the man who had lived quietly in their little town. It should have been payday, but they'd missed him. They'd gotten there just in time to see the golfer escaping in a small plane.

The other thing that bothered him? Well, it didn't really bother him much because it was just his son. Lately, Denny didn't seem to want to be in the same room with him, but that was no big loss. Denny might be a replica of him, but he was so much like his mother in temperament he sometimes made Dennis sick to his stomach. Too bad she hadn't taken Denny with her when she left.

With one last kick at the pile of socks, shorts, and t-shirts, Dennis gave up the search for a cigarette. As for the mess he'd created, he'd let Denny clean it up.

CHAPTER 24

Robert Fox was puzzled. Why was Dennis McCain ignoring him? Robert had to admit that he'd felt a wave of revulsion when Dennis had given him the order to do away with the girl. Had Dennis sensed that? Was that the reason he'd said to him, "Get out of here. I'll take care of this myself"? Whatever the cause, Robert just wanted to thank the man.

Hoping to be the first one to arrive at the rental house, he was surprised to see an old junker in the driveway. Seconds after he'd parked behind it and crawled out of his car, the door of the house flew open and Dennis stepped out.

"Move your car, dumbhead," he snarled at Robert. "You're blocking me."

Robert was surprised about several things....why was he being called a dumbhead, and why was Dennis driving a junker car?

Judging by the look on Dennis' face, Robert's quick decision to ignore the dumbhead remark was a smart one. "Good morning, Dennis. I didn't recognize the car. I don't believe I've ever seen it before."

"Of course you've never seen it before because it's not my car. Do you really think I'd drive a car like that on purpose?"

Robert was too smart to answer that question.

Dennis continued his rant. "Of course I wouldn't! My loser son owns that pile of crap!"

Yipes! What a way to talk about your own kid! "You have a son?"

"If you want to call him that, yes, I have a son, a disgusting goody-goody-do-gooder!"

"Uh," Robert debated asking the question. "Then why are you driving your son's car?"

Dennis' face broke into a broad smile. "That's because my car has an empty gas tank!"

Robert was puzzled by the delighted smile.

Dennis slapped Robert on the back. "Don't you get it? If old-stick-to-the-rules Denny wants to get to his no-account job, he's gonna have to bum a ride, or walk."

"And why would that make you happy?"

Dennis growled. "What are you... a psychiatrist?"

Robert shook his head. "I didn't mean to sound that way, but I find it strange that you'd want to make getting to work difficult for your son. Where does he work?"

"Well, he was flipping burgers at a fast-food restaurant before he got hired by the school board not as a *real* teacher but as a *substitute* teacher. See what I mean? He's never been above being mediocre in anything."

Robert's blue eyes widened. His son was a teacher?

Seeing Robert's reaction, Dennis added, "Yeah, Denny teaches at the same school as Julia. In fact, I met the girl one day when Denny's car wouldn't start. She knew me, and that's the reason I gave you the job of getting rid of her."

Robert's mouth dropped open. "B...b...but...!"

Dennis shook his head. "No, I don't want to know the details."

"B...b...but...!" sputtered Robert.

"I said I didn't want to hear the details! So you took advantage of her before you did the deed? I don't give a shit!"

Dennis turned, stomped back into the house and missed seeing Robert's knees buckle. Feeling as if he'd been punched in the stomach, he staggered back to his car. If Dennis hadn't said, "Get out of here. I'll take care of this myself", then who had? But it *was* Dennis! He had seen him with his own eyes and heard him with his own ears. Was he going crazy?

Driving aimlessly around town wasn't solving anything. Maybe it was time to go back to Ohio, back to wait out the time left on his suspension from the police force. Hell, he wasn't the only cop with sticky fingers; he just had the misfortune of getting caught. Unfortunately, because it was suspension without pay, the easy money the Michigan job had offered was hard to turn down. Too bad the crew that had been sent to do away with the golfer and the lady had gotten there too late. In anticipation of collecting the contract money and getting paid, the celebration had been in full swing. A big banner proclaiming "Mission Accomplished" was quickly torn down when the news came that the targets had flown away in a small plane. He didn't fully understand why the professional golfer had to die, but if the size of the contract meant anything, the golfer had royally pissed off someone.

He might be a cop with no conscience, but even knowing that Julia could identify him, he just couldn't take the job of killing her. But who had? Or worse still, who hadn't?

* * * *

Julia drank the tea like a good girl, she'd eaten all the slices of toast Judy Binder had prepared for her, and she'd slept as many hours as her body could stand. Constant worry about her job, constant concern over putting the Binders in danger, and constant grief over losing her mother had emotionally exhausted her. Then there was Denny, the guy who had put himself in danger by saving her, and now had to stay away from her in case he was being watched.

If both Mom and the Pittsburgh buyer were dead, would she ever find out why someone wanted her dead, too?

CHAPTER 25

"Don't you think it's about time we introduce ourselves?" The question had gotten sidetracked the last time Susan had asked it.

"Sounds like a good idea," Ryan agreed as he tossed a well-chewed apple core over the side of the treehouse.

"No!" cried the girl.

Fast as a monkey, she scampered down the tree, retrieved the core, and in a matter of seconds, was back in the treehouse.

"A dumb trick like that will get us all killed!"

Ryan looked confused. "Wh... wh...what did I do?"

"In order for there to be an apple core, someone had to eat the apple. Right?"

"I get it...I get it!"

"How do you think I've lived here without being discovered?"

"I said I get it!"

Susan waited until the girl had calmed down before she handed the girl what was left of her apple. "So, what do you do with your leavings?" she asked.

"I bury everything," the girl replied. "Look, you two, I have no idea who you are. Maybe you're the bad guys, and maybe you're the good guys…it doesn't matter, because whoever you are, you are going to get me out of here!"

Ryan held up his hand. "Wait a minute!"

Susan butted in. "You wait a minute! We never finished the introduction thing!" Turning to the girl, Susan said, "I'll go first. My name is Susan Cook and I sell residential real estate."

The girl stuck out her hand. "Glad to meet you, Susan. My name is Lynanne James, I'm fifteen years old, and I live in a treehouse."

Ryan squirmed. "It's my turn, isn't it?" he asked Susan. "So, who am I?"

Lynanne's eyes went back to Susan. "What did he mean by that?"

Susan pointed to the bump on Ryan's head. "He…he…he's having trouble remembering. It's some kind of amnesia…we think."

A light went on in Lynanne's eyes. Grabbing the garbage bag, she rummaged around until her hands found what they were looking for. Pulling out the thick book, she opened it to the table of contents. Flipping through the book, her flying fingers found the section she was looking for. "Amnesia, amnesia, amnesia," she muttered as her fingers slid down the page.

"Here it is!'Amnesia: Memory loss that may be caused by a head injury or stroke, substance abuse, or a severe emotional event, such as combat or a motor vehicle accident.' Hmmm. It doesn't mention a plane crash, but that would fit in under a motor vehicle accident, don't you think?" she asked, looking up at Ryan. Without waiting for an answer, she continued. "Now there seems to be seven different types of amnesia. There's anterograde amnesia where a patient cannot remember new information, there's retrograde amnesia where someone will be unable to recall events that occurred before the onset of amnesia. Oh, here's a good one! Transient global amnesia can be caused by an intense orgasm!"

"Wow!" laughed Ryan. "Does it say anything about mind-blowing sex *curing* amnesia?"

Embarrassed, Susan turned her back to him. "She's fifteen," Susan scolded, "What kind of a book is that?"

"It's my mom's medical dictionary."

"And it actually says…what you just said?"

Lynanne giggled. "I sure didn't make that one up! Are you two married?"

Susan shook her head vigorously. "No, I just met the man! I've been a widow for many years."

"If you've just met him, where were you going with him in an airplane?"

Ryan pointed at the bump on his head. "Susan has to tell you the story because I don't remember any of it."

With her eyebrows raised in question, she looked at Ryan. "Do I tell her everything?"

Ryan grinned. "I'd kinda like to hear the story again."

"Well," Susan turned to Lynanne. "I was just trying to sell this man," and she pointed at Ryan, "a house. He told me he was relocating to my area, and every time his work brought him into town, he'd call and make an appointment with me to see houses."

Ryan's eyes casually scanned Susan's body. With a half smile on his face and his eyebrows wriggling like brown caterpillars, he murmured, "I'll bet Charles enjoyed every minute."

Lynanne was confused. "Charles? Who's Charles?"

The playful tone was gone from Ryan's voice when he replied. "According to Susan, my name is Charles, the man flying the plane. After the crash," he pointed to the bump on his head, "I was Ryan when I woke up. But that's not the whole story." Turning to Susan, he said, "Tell her the rest of our adventure."

Susan snorted. "Some adventure! Now, how many days ago was it?" She closed her eyes and counted on her fingers. "I showed Charles a house on Monday. When the hit men showed up, we escaped to his secret house and spent the night. Tuesday morning we flew until we crashed, and we've spent one night here…so today is Wednesday."

"So it's Wednesday! I'm never sure what day it is, but you mentioned bad guys?" Lynanne's eyes were sparkling. "There are bad guys?"

Ryan nudged Susan. "Tell the story from the beginning. Maybe you'll say something that will make me remember."

Susan reached over and touched his head. "Maybe when the lump goes down, your amnesia will disappear. Hey, wait a minute! The roots of your hair are a different color than the rest of your hair!"

Lynanne pointed to the five-o'clock shadow that was growing on Ryan's face. "Look at that! The hair coming in on his face is the same color as his hair roots!"

Susan laughed and poked Ryan in the ribs. "Do blondes really have more fun?"

Ryan grabbed the mirror. "That's why I look so different! I'm not a blonde." He brought the mirror closer to his face. "Hmmm. I don't recall ever having a dimple in my chin. And my nose? Where are the bumps? I played amateur hockey when I was younger...I can't tell you how many times my nose has been broken!"

Lynanne hugged herself. "Oh, this is going to be good! Dyed hair, plastic surgery, different names! I haven't heard a good story....shhhh!"

Men's voices could be heard, first in the distance, and then louder as they came closer to the tree.

Lynanne closed her eyes and quit breathing. Watching her, Susan and Ryan saw real fear. No one moved until the voices no longer could be heard.

Ryan hadn't realized he'd been holding his breath until he let it out. "Lynanne, I promise that I will never throw my apple core...or anything else...on the ground again."

CHAPTER 26

The old junker car was there in the school's parking lot just where Robert Fox expected it to be. He was looking at his watch, wondering what time school let out when he heard the distant sound of the bell. When the school doors flew open and noisy kids of all ages streamed out, Robert drove to the back of the lot and waited.

The teachers came out later, usually several at a time, chatting with each other on the way to their cars. No one paid any attention to Robert who was sitting quietly in a borrowed car. The parking lot was almost empty by the time the door opened and Dennis McCain walked out. Robert was puzzled. Why would Dennis be at his son's school? Then it dawned on him. That wasn't Dennis, that had to be his son. They were almost identical. So it was Dennis' son who had said, "Get out of here. I'll take care of this."

Etched on Robert's memory was that last wretched sight of a bound woman lying in her own excrement. The intense relief he'd felt when Dennis had pushed him aside was being replaced by a feeling of intense doom.

Dennis' wild temper was legendary. Robert had watched him beat a man to death over a minor dispute. It was bad enough that Julia was still a living witness because Robert had been tricked, but how would Dennis react when he found out that his own son had done the tricking? The son had to have known what his dad had ordered him to do; there was no other reason for the son to pretend to be his father. Dare he tell Dennis what his son had done? Robert shuddered just thinking about Dennis' anger. He wouldn't put it past Dennis to get rid of everyone involved…and that included him. When Robert thought of it that way, he made up his mind; he'd take care of both Dennis' son and the girl.

Robert watched the son as he approached the car, keys in his hand, and then, for some reason, he stooped over and picked up something. The keys. The kid just had dropped the keys. Once he was behind the wheel, the engine tried its best not to start. Finally, with the sound of grinding gears, the old junker drove out of the parking lot. Robert waited a few seconds, and then he followed.

* * * *

Don't look…don't look!

Denny kept repeating the words in his head. Shaking from the effort of trying to look casual while his heart was threatening to stop, the key had slipped out of his fingers and slid across the parking lot. While scrambling to pick it up, he'd snuck a peek.

When his class was preparing to leave for the day, Denny had glanced out of his classroom window just in time to see Old Blue Eyes driving into the school's parking lot. So Blue Eyes knew. But how had he figured out that it wasn't Dennis Senior who'd told him he'd take care of Julia? Had he tried to thank Dennis and found out that his dad had no idea what the blue-eyed man was talking about? Did that mean his dad knew that he had taken advantage of the similarity in their looks and rescued Julia? That opened a big can of worms. He had no idea what his dad would do to silence him, or to what extent he would go to make him tell where he had taken Julia.

Old Blue Eyes was probably hoping he would drive straight to Julia. Denny looked into his rearview mirror and saw Old Blue Eyes right behind him; he wasn't even trying to hide the fact that he was back there.

The police station was a half block away when Denny flipped on his turn signal. Through his rearview mirror, he watched the expression on Blue Eye's face change. The last Denny saw of him was the back end of his car as he sped away.

* * * *

Robert Fox hesitated but a moment. Dennis' son didn't have any idea what he was stirring up by getting the local police involved. With luck, he'd talk to one of the dirty cops; they'd soon take care of the kid. But what if he talked to someone not on the payroll?

His Ohio suspension was almost over. Maybe it was time to head back home before Dennis found out what he'd done. Undoubtedly, the description the kid would give the cops would mention his eyes. Robert always knew his unusual blue eyes would be his downfall.

Without even going to his motel room to collect his belongings, he headed for Ohio.

CHAPTER 27

"The skunk was the only funny part of your story," Lynanne complained. With a thoughtful look on her face, she continued."Charles knows why he has a contract on his head, but Ryan doesn't. Charles can fly a plane, but Ryan can't."

Ryan had leaned his head against the trunk of the tree, and with closed eyes, listened to Susan's voice. Suspended between waking and sleeping, he became aware that he was having flashes of recognition. Was he remembering something, or was it just because it was the second time he'd heard the story?

Susan was poking him in the ribs. "Was my story that boring?"

"Wh…wh…what?" Ryan roused himself and looked around. Finding just the two of them, he asked, "Where's Lynanne?"

"Lynanne has gone to the dump to leave her dad a message. Did you really fall asleep?"

Ryan hesitated, and then made a quick decision. Now was not the time to say anything. "No, I don't think I was asleep, but I sure missed the dump thing."

"It seems she and her dad have a way of communicating with each other."

"I don't get it," Ryan remarked. "How has she managed to live out here without getting caught? And did you see how frightened she was when the men walked under the tree?"

Susan looked thoughtful. "We've put her into a dangerous position. One person hiding is one thing; three people hiding...not so good."

"She sees us as a way out of here," Ryan rubbed the bump on his head. "I just wish *we* could see a way out of here!"

Lynanne's head appeared at the edge of the platform. "I should be hearing from Dad pretty soon," she announced as she plopped down beside them.

When both Susan and Ryan looked at her with raised eyebrows, she reached into the pocket of her jacket and pulled out what looked like a phone with a picture of Big Bird on it.

Susan's eyes widened. "Is that what I think it is? I bought one of those for my daughter when she was ten years old."

Ryan looked puzzled.

"It's a walkie-talkie!" Lynanne explained.

"Looks like a toy to me!" Ryan looked at it suspiciously. "A toy keeps you and your dad in contact with each other?"

Lynanne huffed. "Hey, don't knock it! It works!"

Susan nodded in agreement. "I know they work. Julia and her friends had a lot of fun with walkie-talkies. Of course, I suppose all the kids now have cell phones."

"Well, the creeps don't know that we have these. I can't risk calling him, but when I leave a pile of pinecones in a certain part of the dump, he knows to call me. Otherwise, he just leaves packages of food for me in garbage bags."

"Child," Susan moaned, "this is no way for a fifteen-year-old to live!"

Lynanne grinned. "That's why you two are going to get me out of here!"

Ryan studied the girl. "What do you think they'd do to you if they caught you?"

The grin left her face. "I know what they would do to me because I've watched what they do to girls they bring to the farm." She stopped talking and shuddered. "I can show you graves."

"Oh, no!" Susan cried.

"Dad picked this tree because there's rarely any reason for the workers to come to this part of the woods. In the summer, the leaves hide the platform, but in the winter…." Lynanne shrugged and glanced at the leaves that were already turning color. "I made it through last winter without anyone seeing me, but I'm not looking forward to another one."

"And there's no way for the two of you to get out of here?" Ryan questioned.

Lynanne replied quietly, "My dad could probably escape if it were just him, but he doesn't think the two of us could make it out of here without outside help. I worry that something might happen to him, and then…"

"Are you there, girl?"

Lynanne pushed a button and put the instrument to her mouth.

"Hi, Dad!"

"You have something to tell me?"

CHAPTER 28

Dennis looked up from his plate of bacon and eggs and found Mrs. Jack Freed on the other side of the table smiling at him. "You look *so* much like my Jackie when I first met him. Just sitting here with you takes me back to that time and I feel almost young again!"

"Jack must have loved you very much," purred Dennis. "He left you as financially secure as he could at that time, but how long ago was that? Ten years?"

The woman, with tears in her eyes, nodded her head.

Pushing aside his plate, he reached for his briefcase. "Times and opportunities have changed in those ten years! Let me show you what I have done for others who have trusted me to invest their money."

One glance at the chart that he handed to her, and the woman gushed, "Oh, my goodness! Can you do that for me?"

Dennis looked away. It would never do for the mark to see the eyes of the predator going in for the kill.

Later that day, he was pulling into a parking place outside the rented house when the door flew open and Lloyd, one of the pretend cops, rushed out before Dennis could get out of the car.

"Something wrong?"

"I told that blue-eyed son-of-a-bitch he could borrow my car if he brought it right back. That was hours ago! Have you seen him?"

"I'm happy to say that I haven't. He's been acting squirrelly lately. Have you noticed?"

"Squirrelly? How so?"

"He's been like a love-sick kid around me. I can do without his hugs."

"Oh, that. I think he was trying to say thank-you for something you did for him."

"Something I did for him? Like what?"

"I don't know, but it had something to do with the girl."

Dennis snorted. "The kid's sick. It makes me wonder if he messed with her before or after he killed her. I really don't give a shit one way or another. Just so she's eliminated."

"Robert killed Julia? I don't think so. He was sweet on her."

"I gave him an order! Of course he killed her!"

"Well, when he comes back with my car, you can ask him yourself."

Dennis muttered to himself as he went into the house. "Of course he killed her."

* * * *

From her bedroom window, Julia gazed with mixed emotions at the house next door. It was the only house Julia had ever lived in, but now the dark empty-eyed windows that looked back at her made the house seem unwelcoming. It was the same house, but without her mother in it, her feelings toward it had changed. Her mother should be in there, waiting with open arms to greet her. But she wasn't there and never would be again. Julia put her forehead against the cold windowpane and cried. What kind of trouble had dragged both her mother and her Pittsburgh buyer to their death?

With her eyes closed, Julia tried to remember the details of her mother's face. When was the last time she had actually looked at her? She was just her mother, for heaven's sake, someone who was always there when she needed her, and Julia never doubted that she would *always* be there when she needed her. And now she was dead. The full impact of death hit her like a sledgehammer. Dead was forever.

Had she aged and Julia hadn't noticed? She needed something of her mother's to hold onto…she needed…she needed… a picture…yes, that was it, she needed a picture. Then she remembered. On Thanksgiving Day, she had taken pictures with her iPhone. She had sent the pictures by e-mail to her mom's computer, and together they had watched her mom's printer spit them out. The last time she had seen them, they were laying on top of the television set.

Seeing an approaching car in the distance, Julia stepped back from the window and waited for it to pass the house. After all, if she was supposed to be dead, she couldn't run the risk of being seen at the Binders. Putting them in danger was the last thing she wanted to do.

Back at the window, her eyes sought out her old room. Mom hadn't changed a thing in it, so Julia closed her eyes and pretended. Mentally she went through her drawers, sorting through her possessions, and touching them in her mind. Finished with the drawers, she opened the closet doors and inspected each outfit hanging there, finding many outfits that were much better than the ones Judy Binder was lending her.

Her eyes flew open at a daring thought. Why couldn't she run through the backyard and go into her house? She could grab a couple of outfits, and the pictures from the top of the television set. Wait! If she showed up with new outfits, then Judy and Joe would know that she had put them in danger; she settled for just the picture. There was a hidden key in the potted plant by the door; she could be in, grab a picture, and be out before anyone missed her.

CHAPTER 29

Ryan and Susan listened to Lynanne's conversation with her father. Lynanne's dad wasn't too happy about having two more people to hide and feed. If they were caught, all three of them would share the same fate; the workers had no idea he had a daughter. Lynanne was trying to put a positive spin on having two outsiders who, she was sure, would find a way out and take her with them. The walkie-talkie crackled with static and other voices.

"Gotta go, honey!" her dad whispered. "Keep your unit open!"

It always hurt when her infrequent contact with her dad was over. With the receiver in her hand, she sat quietly until Ryan cleared his throat.

She raised her head. "What?"

"We were just wondering about dinner."

"Oh."

Susan was concerned. "Are you all right?" she asked the girl.

Lynanne managed to say, "I'm fine," before she burst into tears.

When Susan wrapped her arms around the girl, she pulled away. "I'm really all right. I don't get to talk to him very often, and when I do, I never want him to end the call." She paused to wipe her eyes on her arm. "To answer your question, Dad takes the garbage to the dump after he feeds them dinner. I don't have a watch, so I have no idea what time that is. I just wait for darkness so no one will see me."

"Speaking of getting dark…it's soon going to be bedtime. How do you handle that?" Susan asked.

Lynanne gave one last sniffle. "Further up this tree, Dad built me a shelter with a roof. I have a sleeping bag in a waterproof container and extra clothes. But first, I go to the stream and wash up. Wanna go with me?" she asked Susan.

"In cold water? Brrr!" Susan shivered. "I don't have any clothes except what I have on, but I could stand a little cleaning up. Do you have soap?"

"Of course I have soap!" laughed the girl. "You think I'm not civilized?"

Ryan chimed in. "You wouldn't have a couple of extra toothbrushes, would you?"

Lynanne shrugged. "I wouldn't be surprised if Dad throws some extra things in with the food."

* * * *

Later, after a dinner of chunks of homemade bread and fried chicken, Lynanne and Susan picked their way through the dark woods to the stream. Along with towels and soap, Lynanne carried a clean change of clothes. She stepped behind a bush, removed her clothes, then all Susan saw was a white streak running past her to the stream. She heard a sudden intake of breath when Lynanne hit the cold water and immediately saw a flurry of soap bubbles. Within a matter of minutes, Lynanne was out of the water, making a mad dash for the bush and the towel.

"Wow!" exclaimed Susan. "That was the fastest bath I've ever seen. Now, I suppose it's my turn?"

Lynanne laughed. "Bet you can't beat my time!"

Susan did more than take a sudden breath when the cold water hit her body, but knowing she couldn't scream, she stifled her reaction.

She didn't break Lynanne's record.

They were about to leave when the sound of something crashing through the weeds made them both run for cover.

"Hey!" Ryan whispered, "It's just me. Can I borrow a towel and the soap?"

"Jesus!" Lynanne gasped.

Susan put her arms around the girl. "You're shaking!"

Sobbing, Lynanne hid her face on Susan's chest. "I...I...I thought...."

"Shhhh," murmured Susan. "It's just Ryan."

"I know, but it was just like the nightmares I have."

"You have bad dreams?"

Lynanne sobbed. "I know that it's going to happen. One day, I'll be down here at the stream, and one of the workers is going to see me...and that will be the end of m...m...me!"

Susan held the shaking girl while murmuring comforting words. For a brief moment, the fifteen-year-old girl in her arms turned into Julia. How often she had comforted her daughter just like this. And if this were Julia, how hard would she fight to get her back into civilization? Suddenly, it became important to find a way out of here, not just for her and Ryan, but also for Lynanne.

Her thoughts were interrupted by the sound of a nearby plane taking off.

"Quick!" Lynanne squealed. "Out of the water, Ryan!"

Grabbing Susan, the girl pushed her into deep foliage.

As the three of them looked up and watched the plane gain altitude, Lynanne remarked, "That's how they get the stuff out of here."

Ryan's eyes followed the plane. According to Susan, he knew how to fly one of those. His hand went up to the bump on his head.

It would have been impossible for the two of them to have found the tree in the dark if Lynanne hadn't been with them. She scampered up to the platform ahead of them while Ryan reached down from the first branch and pulled Susan into the tree. Once on the platform, there was nothing to do but look at each other.

"The day ends when the sun goes down," Lynanne remarked. "There's nothing to do but sleep."

Susan looked around. "So, if your sleeping quarters in this fancy hotel are higher in the tree, do Ryan and I sleep here?"

"That's the plan. I do hope that neither of you is a sleepwalker," Lynanne smirked.

Ryan ran his tongue over his teeth. "When do you talk to your dad again?"

"Anytime I put out the pinecones. You want something?"

Ryan nodded. "Toothbrushes!"

Lynanne hit her forehead with the back of her hand. Reaching around the tree, she pulled out a garbage bag, rummaged through it, and came out with two toothbrushes and a big tube of paste.

"How long have you had these?" Ryan cried.

"Calm down," Lynanne chided. "Jeez. The two of you and toothbrushes! These were in today's bag, so quit bellyaching. I suppose the next thing you're going to ask for is my thermos of water, so here, take the thermos, and take my little shovel. "

"And where are we taking the shovel?" asked Ryan who was as excited about his toothbrush as most kids are about toys on Christmas morning.

"You two are going to climb down the tree, go some distance away from the tree, brush your teeth, spit out the paste, and use the shovel to bury the evidence."

Lynanne listened to the two of them giggling like kids as they raced through the dark.

"Hey, you two!" she whispered loudly. "Knock off the noise!"

She wondered if they were aware of the current running between the two of them. She could feel it, but had they recognized it? They were still laughing when they climbed back up the tree.

"Okay," Lynanne paused in her ascent to her sleeping quarters. "Time for bed. If either of you have to relieve yourself before morning…well, you're on your own." With that she disappeared.

"Gee, I wish she hadn't said that," grimaced Ryan. "Now all I can think about is how badly I have to go."

"You did drink a lot of water today. We don't even know if the water in the stream is drinkable."

Ryan paused in his progress down the tree. "Lynanne looks healthy. Hey, I'll be back in a minute."

Keeping their tree in sight, Ryan was preparing to relieve himself when he heard voices approaching. Damn! Where should he go? The voices, coming in his direction, were getting closer. Trying to be quiet, he crept deeper into the woods, putting distance between him and the voices.

Long minutes passed before Ryan felt safe to release the breath he'd been holding.

After relieving himself, he looked around for their tree. In the dark, all the trees looked alike. With growing apprehension, he realized he had no idea where he was.

Susan waited a bit for Ryan to return, but it had been a long and stressful day. Wrapped in the fur coat, she lay down to await his return, but instead, fell fast asleep.

* * * *

The forest was alive with animal sounds greeting the dawn when Lynanne shook her awake.

"Where's Ryan?" she barked.

"Wh...wh...what?" Susan grumbled.

"Wake up!" Lynanne insisted. "Where's Ryan?"

Susan sat up and looked around. She was still wrapped in the coat that they should have been sharing.

"He didn't come back!" she cried.

"Back from where?" There was panic in Lynanne's voice.

"He...he had to relieve himself. The last thing I remember, he was climbing down the tree, telling me he'd be right back. What could have happened to him?"

"Lots!" Lynanne grimaced. "I'll bet they caught him."

"What will they do to him? Kill him?" Susan wailed.

"Probably try to get him to confess that he's a federal agent."

Susan cried, "But he's not!"

Lynanne shrugged. "So he's not. That doesn't matter to them; they'll kill him, anyway. I can show you graves."

Susan sobbed. "What can we do?"

"Nothing," the girl said grimly. "Don't you *dare* even think about trying to find him because they'll grab you, too. Then I'll hide up here in my tree and watch them bury both of you."

Susan threw her hands over her face. For the first time since the crash, she felt desperate. Even though the crash had put the two of them in serious trouble, there was something about Ryan that had made her feel safe. She didn't know why, he just did.

"Lynanne, where are we?"

The girl looked puzzled. "We're right here!"

Susan almost chuckled. "No, I mean what state are we are in. Charles...remember that's who was flying the plane...wouldn't tell me where we were going, and of course, after the crash when Charles turned into Ryan, he didn't know, either."

"We're in Georgia, just south of the Tennessee border. I'm surprised you didn't ask me before."

"I guess things have just happened too fast. I'd been showing Charles houses long enough to feel comfortable around him, but Ryan...that was one big shock...to both of us."

Lynanne was thinking. "Remember the story you told about your using your cell phone, and the organization that's after Charles traced the call?"

"Yes, and I can't tell you how awful I felt! I looked out the airplane window and watched his house and barn burn."

"Do you think they could trace you here?"

"Probably, but why would I want them to?"

Lynanne shrugged. "Can you think of a way we could use your phone that maybe could get us out of here?"

"The only ones who would be tracing my phone would be the ones who want to collect on the contract. But they'd come here to kill Ryan. That's not what you're thinking, is it?"

Lynanne shook her head. "No, no! I like Ryan. But if they did come, the workers might think they're federal agents. If they thought that, they'd fight to the death, They hate those agents."

"Hmmm." Susan wrinkled her forehead. "How could we be sure they'd think the intruders were agents?"

Lynanne grinned, "My dad could see to that."

"Would he do that?"

"Hey, they're holding him captive! He can't get that alarm thing off his leg! Of course he'd do it!"

"Could this work?" Susan mused. "It's such a wild plan, who would agree to go along with it?"

"Let's keep it simple cause I have to explain it to Dad."

"Here's what I'm thinking. If you can get your dad to spread rumors that he'd run into evidence that the feds have been nosing around, the workers would get ready to fight. Then when the organization trying to get rid of Charles/Ryan arrives, the two groups will kill each other! How's that for a crazy plan?" Susan laughed.

"Dad doesn't usually go for crazy things," Lynanne replied, " but he sure wants to get out of here."

Susan sighed. "There's one hitch."

"What's that?"

"Besides the fact that, right now, I have the cell phone and Ryan has the battery in his pocket, I've already tried use my cell. My phone didn't connect with a tower."

"Oh." Lynanne sounded as if the air had been let out of her balloon.

CHAPTER 30

Signs of dawn lighting up the eastern sky found an exhausted Ryan stretched out under a tree. How could he have been so stupid? Instead of calmly trying to work his way back to where he'd been when he heard the voices, he had panicked. All night long he had stumbled from tree to tree, never finding the right one. His mouth was dry, he was covered with scratches from running into thorny vegetation, and he was scared. What if one of the workers found him? Lynanne's stories of what happened to outsiders made him reconsider falling asleep on the ground. Reluctantly, he roused himself, found a tree, and climbed it.

A fork halfway up the tree allowed him to wedge his body, making him feel safe enough to close his eyes.

He was asleep when a man on a small tractor filled with garbage bags passed underneath the tree.

The sun was high in the sky when the sound of an airplane's sputtering start worked its way into Ryan's dream. As the plane's engine revved up in preparation for take-off, his hands were on the control column, his eyes were checking the instruments, and his heart was beating with excitement. Flying was exhilarating! Feeling confident and in control, he pulled back on the joystick…and woke to find himself wedged into a tree that bordered a landing strip. The memory of being lost last night was as jarring as the sound of the small plane taking off. Fragments of his dream still remained, and the fact that, in his dream, he knew how to fly the plane wasn't surprising…until he remembered that he didn't know how to fly a plane.

With the departure of the plane, the few workers who had watched the plane take off disappeared into the woods. Ryan waited a bit before he pulled himself free of the wedge in the tree and climbed higher hoping he'd see something familiar. If he could find either the stream or the burned plane, he was sure he could find his way to their tree. How embarrassed should he be for getting lost? He was surprised at how much he wanted Susan to think well of him.

Almost to the top of the tree, he stopped and looked around. He saw a farmhouse in the distance, a greenhouse, and fields. He had seen marijuana plants before, so he recognized the crop. His eyes scanned the surrounding area and landed on a place where the woods thinned; it was the only break in the sea of trees. Could that be the clearing where Charles had tried to land the plane?

Working his way down the tree, he kept his ears and eyes alert. The last thing he wanted to do was to run into a worker. Hungry, thirsty, and apprehensive, Ryan, used the sun as a guide and started the journey to the clearing.

∗ ∗ ∗ ∗

Susan could hear Lynanne crashing through the trees before she saw her. It was obvious that she was trying to run, but the garbage bag she had flung over her back was slowing her down. Susan didn't like the way the girl kept looking back over her shoulder. Was someone chasing her? She scampered down the tree part way and was there to catch the bag when Lynanne threw it up to her.

"Go! Go!" whispered Lynanne.

It wasn't until both of them were high in the tree that Lynanne took a relieved breath.

"Man, that was close!" she whispered, pointing.

Four workmen, talking and laughing, passed underneath their tree.

Lynanne was shaking. "I thought they saw me!"

"I can't believe you've lived like this for a year!"

With her eyes closed, Lynanne waited for her heart to stop pounding. Opening her eyes, she pointed at Susan. "That's why you have to get me out of here. I figure it's just a matter of time before they find me!"

Susan threw up her hands. "With Ryan gone, I feel helpless!"

"Get over it!" Lynanne begged. "If they've captured him, he's never coming back!"

Never coming back? The thought tied Susan's stomach in a knot. She had been impressed with Charles the gentleman, but it was Ryan the playboy who had gotten under her skin; it hurt to admit to herself how deep her feelings were for him. Did he know? Those moments in the warm embrace of the fur coat had reminded her of what she'd been missing all those years. Never coming back?

Trying to hide her anxiety from the girl, Susan nudged the garbage bag with her foot. "Anything interesting in there?"

Lynanne grinned. "Breakfast, and Dad threw in a few other things."

Indeed, there were other things... a hairbrush, shampoo, and several clean towels.

Spreading the food out on napkins, Lynanne wondered aloud. "Do we save some for Ryan in case he finds his way back?"

"Listen!" Susan hissed.

The sound of a small motor in the distance kept getting louder until out of the trees came a tractor with a load of full garbage bags.

"Dad!" Lynanne breathed.

Lynanne's dad put a finger over his lips and shook his head. The tractor slowed down enough to allow Ryan to push his way from under a pile of bags and roll to the ground. The tractor picked up speed and disappeared.

Watching him scramble up the tree, Susan's heart surged with feelings so strong her legs didn't want to support her.

Without saying a word, he gathered her into his arms and held her so close she could feel his heart pounding.

"Oh, Ryan!" Susan murmured.

"Don't talk, just hold me," Ryan pleaded.

Lynanne watched the two adults clinging to each other. The current she had felt running between the two of them was stronger than ever. Ryan was crying and whispering into Susan's ear. Whatever he was saying to Susan, she wasn't objecting.

Lynanne waited patiently for them; she was dying to hear how her dad had gotten into the picture. When Lynanne's demanding questions finally got their attention, Susan's feeble attempt to step out of the embrace only made Ryan pull her closer.

"You want to know what happened?" he asked, looking at Lynanne over Susan's head.

"Yes! How did you end up with my dad?"

Holding on to Susan, Ryan told his story that ended with him lying flat on his stomach drinking water at the stream when her dad had driven up on the tractor. Ryan had thought all was lost until the driver identified himself.

"Where did you spend the night?" Susan wondered.

"In a tree. I woke up to the noise of a plane taking off." Looking pleased with himself, he announced, "I found the landing strip!"

"That's how I want to leave this place," Lynanne stated. "I want to get on one of those planes and fly out of here!"

Susan shrugged. "It doesn't matter what you want. How could anything like that happen?"

Lynanne pointed at Ryan. "He knows how to fly."

Ryan closed his eyes, remembering his dream. "Strange for you to say that, because the sound of the plane getting ready to take off worked its way into my dream. I was checking all the dials, and holding the joystick in my hand, knowing everything I needed to know to fly the plane."

"See, I knew it! You just have to become Charles again!"

Ryan laughed. "That would be a good trick if you could make it happen. Any ideas?"

Lynanne muttered as she pulled a garbage bag open and pulled out her medical book. "I'm going up to my sleeping quarters to study. Anyhow, you two look like you need to be alone." From her climb up the tree, she paused and called down, "Ryan, you can have my share of breakfast."

With Lynanne gone, Ryan suddenly felt awkward holding Susan. Dropping his arms, he stepped back. "I...I...I don't know what came over me," he said to her. "It's just that I was so sca...."

Susan held her breath. Was he going to pretend that he hadn't said those things to her? "Ryan," she breathed out the words. "Please, *please* don't apologize."

"I'm not apologizing!" Ryan protested. "As long as we were together, I knew that we were in a pretty scary situation, but somehow the two of us would find a way out of it." With a catch in his voice, he added, "And then I couldn't find my way back to you."

Susan threw herself into his arms. With her face buried in his chest, she sobbed. "Oh, Ryan... I felt...I felt...when you didn't come back...I felt..!"

Ryan's arms closed around her. "Shhh," he whispered. Bending his head, he looked into her eyes. "Charles the gentleman probably wouldn't do this, but I'm not Charles."

Engrossed in her medical book's section on amnesia, Lynanne could faintly hear Susan and Ryan's voices. Just having someone to talk to was great, plus there were so many intriguing facets to these two. Being chased by hit men, plastic surgery, bleached hair, amnesia...she squirmed with anticipation; they were going to get her out of here.

Curious at the sudden silence, she leaned over and looked down at the two people on the platform. They were kissing. She was grinning until she remembered the details of the case she had just read. The subject of the study was a man who had fallen in love during his amnesia period. When his memory came back, so did the knowledge that he was married to someone else.

Dare she look down again? A quick peek brought the sight of Susan and Ryan lying down on the platform, completely covered by the fur coat. She could the sound of kisses mixed in with bouts of crying and soft murmurings. Lynanne hid her red face behind the pages of the thick medical book.

CHAPTER 31

Denny watched the blue-eyed cop's car disappear in traffic. Relieved, he drove past the police station without slowing down. Not knowing who in the police force he could trust, he wasn't about to work with any of them.

What did the blue-eyed cop want from him? Knowing what his dad did to anyone who messed up on one of his orders, Old Blue Eye's best move would be to get out of town...and stay out of town. On the other hand, the cop might figure that if he could find out where Julia was hidden, he could get back in good standing with Dennis. Was that the reason he'd shown up at school?

Driving around aimlessly, Denny had nowhere to go. Could he ever go home again? If his dad had figured out that Julia was still alive because his own son had rescued her....

Denny felt as if someone had punched him in the stomach. Could he even show up for work tomorrow? With both the blue-eyed cop and his dad looking for him, where could he hide? Who could he trust?

Honking horns roused him from his pondering; the red light had turned green. Giving the driver behind him an apologetic wave, he glanced around as he sped away. His aimless driving had taken him to the area where the Binders lived. In case someone was following him, he knew he shouldn't drive down the street where he had taken Julia, but it did make him think of the house next to the Binders. Julia's mother, Susan, was dead; her house was vacant. It was such an obvious place to hide and that would make it a dangerous place to hide. Knowing his dad, Denny figured Susan's house would be the first place he'd check. He shrugged in resignation; there was nowhere else. As if to remind him that his car was going to be a problem, the engine shuddered. Some cars you could hide, but not a junker like his.

There had to be a place he could leave his car without calling attention to it. A junk yard would work nicely, but there weren't any of those within the city limits. Then Denny had a brilliant idea.

* * * *

Julia waited until after the dinner dishes had been washed and put away before she casually mentioned that she was retiring early.

"Are you not feeling well?" Judy Binder looked worried. "Your favorite show is on tonight, and I thought we could watch it together."

Julia hesitated. It *was* her favorite show. Drat. The Binders had accepted her into their lives without any hesitation. The least she could do was watch the show with Judy. She'd sneak next door after they went to bed. Later was probably better, anyway.

"I'd forgotten what night it was! Guess I'll go to bed after the show."

Judy gave her a hug. "Good! I'll make some popcorn to eat while we watch it."

* * * *

It was a two-mile hike from the used car lot to Susan's house. By the time Denny got there, the Binder house was dark except for one lighted upstairs window. He was watching it, wondering if that was Julia's room, when the light went out. Julia was probably going to bed.

Now that he was outside Susan's house he wasn't sure how he was going to get inside. He momentarily considered breaking a window, but if anyone came around the house they'd definitely notice that. Plus, Denny wasn't much of a vandal, and the thought of destroying Julia's home was unsettling. Hoping that Julia or her mother had hidden a key somewhere around the house, Denny began a silent search for one. He was down on his knees, feeling around for anything that felt like a key, when he became aware of a slight figure approaching from the direction of the Binder house. Denny stepped into the shadow and held his breath. Whoever it was, they knew to look in the potted plant for the key.

"Julia?" he whispered.

She screamed, piercing the night with a shrill sound of terror.

"Shhhh! It's me...Denny!" he said stepping into the light waving his arms.

"Oh, my God!" Sobbing, Julia collapsed into Denny's arms, tears streaming down her cheeks.

"You're shaking! I'm so sorry I scared you!"

"I...I...I thought ...."

"I know what you thought!"

Julia continued to sob.

Denny held her until she was no longer shaking.

"You okay now?" he asked.

Julia gave one last sob. "That was the worst scare of my life!"

"I'm so sorry! I apologize again for upsetting you."

Julia peered at him through the darkness. "Why are you here?" she asked her voice huskier than usual. Her throat was raw from the scream and from the days of crying herself to sleep.

"I could ask you the same question. You're taking a chance you know. You're supposed to be dead."

"I asked you first."

"Could you please use the key that's in your hand and open the door? I'll tell you all about it once we're inside."

Neither one spoke a word until they were standing in the entryway of Susan's house. There was enough illumination coming from nightlights for Julia to see the alarmed look on Denny's face.

"Are you trying to get yourself killed?" he hissed.

Julia hung her head.

"And Joe and Judy? Have you any idea…."

Julia interrupted. "Please stop!"

"I'm not stopping until you get it into your head that you're still in danger!"

To Denny's surprise, Julia threw herself into his arms.

"Whoa!" Denny exclaimed after he regained his balance. "I…I'm sorry I yelled at you….I guess."

Julia howled, "Mom's dead!"

"Yes she is, and I am so sorry! But you found that out days ago."

"I know," she gulped. "But the fact just hit me that dead is forever!" In a mournful voice, she wailed, "I can't remember what Mom looked like!"

"Oh!" Confused, he asked, "But you were home recently! Remember the convertible?"

"But I didn't really look at her! I mean, *really* look at her. You don't have to pay much attention to your mother because she's always going to be there…I thought!"

Denny didn't say anything. Since he hadn't seen his own mother for years, he actually couldn't remember what she looked like. His dad had destroyed all the pictures of the wife who had left him.

Julia gave a nervous little laugh when she realized that she was still holding on to Denny. Stepping back, she wiped her face on the sleeve of her jacket before she said, "I need a picture of my mom. That's what I came for."

"You risked three lives for a picture?"

"Okay, so it was a dumb reason. Is your reason any better? Why are you here in my mom's house?"

"I'm hiding."

Julia gasped. "Hiding? Who's after you?"

"A couple of people. My dad found out that I rescued you by pretending to be him, so when he realizes that I'm not coming home, he'll come looking for me. I'm sure he thinks that if he finds me, he'll also find you. And then there's Old Blue Eyes who's in trouble with my dad because I tricked him…he was waiting for me in the school's parking lot today."

"What does he want?"

"The same thing my dad wants."

"And that is?"

"Me," he said shrugging, "and you."

"Me?" Julia squeaked.

"Yes, you! That's why you can't take chances! You can identify too many people."

Julia got quiet. "So, are you going to live here in Mom's house until this all blows over?"

Denny nodded.

"What about our jobs?"

"Let's not even think about our jobs. If we lose them, maybe we'll have to apply to teach in another school district…or maybe Mrs. Sheldon will listen to our stories and take us back."

Leaving Denny in the foyer, Julia walked into the dark kitchen and opened the refrigerator door.

"No!" shouted Denny. Racing into the kitchen, he slammed the door shut.

Jumping back, Julia cried, "What was all that about?"

"When the rest of the house is dark, the light from the refrigerator can be seen from outside. Why were you looking in there in the first place? Don't the Binders feed you?"

"Of course they feed me! I was just wondering if Mom had anything in the refrigerator that you could eat."

"I hadn't thought about eating," Denny admitted. "Maybe I should just stick to stuff in the pantry and open the refrigerator door only during the day."

Julia looked around her home and sighed. What was going to become of this house? Did Mom have a will? If she did, the house would become hers. Julia shook her head; there's no way she could even pay the taxes on this house. She'd have to clean it out, give all her mother's personal things to Goodwill, and then put the house on the market. She was sure there would be someone in her mom's real estate office that would handle it for her.

With the pictures clutched in one hand, Julia squared her shoulders and readied herself to sneak back across the yard. Pausing at the door, she stopped, thought for a moment, and then ran back to Denny and hugged him.

"Thank you again for saving me," she whispered.

* * * *

Dennis Sr. sat in his dark house and waited. He hadn't decided what he was going to do to Denny to make him talk, but he had no doubt that he would. Any minute now, he was going to walk through the front door. After all, Denny had a responsible teaching job, and his stick-to-the-rules boring son would want to get a good night's sleep.

If Robert Fox had returned the borrowed car, Dennis would never have known what his son had done. But Robert hadn't, and Lloyd, the owner of the car, was so angry that he broke his sworn oath not to tell. Out there, still alive, was a witness who could identify too many of the local people who had been lured to the dark side by the smell of easy money. Denny was going to tell him where he had hidden Julia, and this time he wouldn't ask someone else to do the job. He'd take care of it himself.

With his eyes fixed on the luminous face of the clock, he watched the minute hand that seemed to be moving slower and slower....

Light was shining through the windows when the ringing of his cell phone jarred him awake. Confused, he fumbled around, trying to find and stop the unsettling noise.

"Hello?" he growled.

"Mr. McCain?"

"Yeah."

"This is Mrs. Sheldon. Is there some reason you haven't shown up at school?"

"Uh, this is Dennis Senior. I think you're looking for Dennis Junior."

"Oh, I'm sorry, Mr. McCain! I see now I made a mistake. I have two phone numbers and they are clearly marked Senior and Junior. By the way, did anyone ever tell you that you and your son sound alike?"

"Yeah, I think it has been mentioned once or twice."

"Well, I have a class of eighth graders who are without a teacher. Is your son around?"

"No, he isn't."

There was silence on the other end.

"Well, at this late date I don't have much chance of finding a substitute. If you see your son, would you please tell him to call the school?"

Dennis grunted and hung up. What do you know? His stick-to-the-rules son hadn't come home last night, and his stick-to-the-rules son hadn't shown up for work this morning. Dennis scratched his bristly jaw. As far as he knew, Denny didn't have friends…at least he never brought any to the house, so where did he spend the night? As for girls, he'd never known Denny to date. But what about that girl, Julia? Dennis had to admit that his son had shown unexpected inventiveness in rescuing her.

Feeling the need for coffee, he wandered into the kitchen and stared at the empty pot. Denny always made the morning coffee. Damn kid! Where was he?

Dennis grabbed his car keys and headed for the door. He'd stop for coffee at a drive-through on his way to search for Denny's crappy car. Finding the car would be the first step in finding Julia. He'd bet his last dollar that when he found Denny, he'd find Julia.

CHAPTER 32

Dennis McCain had patience, but the search for his son's rattletrap of a car had just about used it all. If he hadn't been absolutely convinced that Denny had hidden his car, he would have given up the search hours ago. The car would look right at home in the junk yard but he'd quickly ruled out that location. He needed his search to stay within the city limits because wherever Denny had stowed his car, it had to be within walking distance of…what? The girl?

Of course, the girl. He'd been tackling this from the wrong end. Pulling to the curb, he opened the glove compartment and pulled out a map of the city. Since he had been one of the men who had followed the golfer to the realtor's house that night, he had no trouble finding the street. But he wasn't sure of the house. Wait a minute! The memory of entering the realtor's garage made him smile. It had been full of real estate signs, and the name on the sign was…Cook. Yes, Susan Cook.

With a pencil, Dennis made a circle around the area. If he could find Denny's wreck within the circle, then Julia was somewhere on that street.

Within fifteen minutes, Dennis found the used car lot where the rattletrap was parked. It was the only car on the lot that didn't have a tag on the windshield displaying the asking price. Grinning at his genius, he found a phone book in the back-of-the-seat pocket and looked up Susan Cook's address.

* * * *

Denny was restless. Lying low in the house, staying away from windows, and not turning on lights was getting tedious. Susan had shelves full of romance novels, biographies, and real estate books, and these he read during the day. At night, there was not much he could do but sleep. It amused him to think that with a few more days of studying, he probably could pass the real estate exam.

Something else was making him restless. Knowing that just a short distance separated him from Julia was making him crazy. True, she was treating him as if he were her brother, but if he had a chance he was sure he could change her mind. He'd like to call her on the landline phone, but he couldn't take the chance that Susan's phone wasn't tapped. His own cell phone was down to one bar and he didn't have a charger. Something told him to save the one bar for an emergency.

It was what would have been the dinner hour if there had been any dinner involved, and in Denny's case, there wasn't, when he heard the sound of a car pulling into Susan's driveway.

Standing to the side of the window, he was able to get a glimpse of a very familiar car and a very familiar man getting out of the car. His dad. How in the hell had his dad found him? He had to hide. Wait a minute…his dad wasn't looking at Susan's house…he was staring at the Binder house.

This was the emergency for which Denny had saved the one bar. Thankful that he'd put the Binders' phone number on speed dial, he hit the screen and waited impatiently.

Joe answered. "Hello?"

"Joe, don't say anything…just listen. This is Denny. My dad just pulled into Susan's driveway, but he's looking at your house. Don't be fooled into thinking that it's me ringing your doorbell, because it's not. Dad's an evil man! He's the one who ordered Julia killed. Get rid of anything that looks like Julia might be there, and hide her. And remember, don't be fooled by him. Oh, and don't answer the door until you and Judy come up with some kind of plan!" Denny hung up when, over the phone, he heard the doorbell ring.

Denny stood by the side of the window and watched his dad impatiently punching the doorbell. Finally, after a couple of minutes, a smiling Joe answered the door. When he made a sweeping motion with his arm, Denny yelled, "No!" Was he inviting his dad into the house? It looked as if Dennis was going to take Joe up on his invitation until Judy's happy face appeared beside her husband. Her beaming countenance was sending the message that the biggest thrill of her life would be a visit from this complete stranger. Wait! Did Judy actually plant a kiss on his dad's cheek? What in the world were the Binders up to?

Denny heaved a sigh of relief when he saw his dad beginning to back away from the over-welcoming couple. The Binders stepped out of their house and continued to talk excitedly to their visitor until he backed into his car, fumbled for the door handle and, ignoring the couple who were now wildly waving, burned rubber backing out of the driveway.

It was only a minute before Denny's cell phone rang. He knew it would be the Binders wanting to know how he knew Dennis was in Susan's driveway. From his perch beside the window, he peeked and saw Joe Binder with the phone by his ear, staring at Susan's house. Denny didn't answer his phone.

* * * *

Stupid people! Dennis huffed as he sped away from the neighborhood. How people as dumb as those two managed to live as long as they had was a mystery to him. Uncle Earl? They thought he was their Uncle Earl. Reaching up with the palm of his hand, he rubbed his cheek to remove the saliva left from a sloppy kiss. The enthusiasm of their greeting had so bowled him over he quite forgot why he was there. Their chatter of aunts, uncles, cousins, and in-laws, ended with their quizzing him about the amount of the estate a recently deceased relative had left behind. But it was the completely blank look on their faces when he mentioned the name Julia that had him backing away and fleeing for his life. Maybe Julia was somewhere in the area, but it sure wasn't at those idiots' house!

His foot eased up on the accelerator. Maybe the girl wasn't at that house, but since he was sure he had settled on the right neighborhood, he just had to be patient. Sooner or later either his son or the girl was going to show up. A fleeting thought about Susan Cook's actual house being the place to look was just that; a fleeting thought. Even his dumb son was smart enough not to do something as obvious as that.

CHAPTER 33

Susan and Ryan were snuggling under the fur coat when Lynanne returned with breakfast. The temperature had dropped during the night and Lynanne was sporting a down-filled parka.

Poking her head out, Susan exclaimed, "Wow! It's cold! I can see my breath!"

Ryan's arm sneaked out and pulled her back under. "And for that reason, we're going to spend the rest of the day in here where it's warm!"

Susan giggled.

Lynanne rolled her eyes. "Come on, you guys! We've got work to do!"

"It's too cold to work," was Ryan's muffled reply.

"Dad sent winter jackets and a thermos of hot coffee to go with our eggs and toast."

"Coffee?" Susan's head popped out. "Count me in!"

Lynanne handed her a jacket. "Dad wants to know if you have any way of getting in touch with the outside world."

Susan stopped in the middle of putting on the jacket to give Lynanne a puzzled look. "How does he think we could do that?"

"He was asking about a cell phone. Do you have one?"

Shivering while zipping up the coat, Susan nodded. "You know I have one. Remember we had a conversation about it? But it's useless."

"What do you mean it's useless. You mean it's not charged?"

"Oh, it's charged! I tried right after we crashed, but there was no service available."

"That's strange. I see the workers using theirs, but come to think about it, it's always in a certain high area."

Susan was getting excited. "If that's the case, then I'll bet it would work up here in the tree. Ryan, please give me the battery!"

"Wait, please wait!" Lynanne was so excited she was dancing. "Remember you said that if you turn on your phone, the killers chasing Ryan could trace the call and find where he is?"

Nodding her head, Susan shut her eyes and remembered looking down at his burning house and barn. She had caused that by phoning her daughter.

"We want them to come, but not before my dad plants some evidence that the feds are watching. Then the whole camp will be armed to the teeth."

Ryan was listening intently. "So when the killers come after Charles the two groups will fight each other?"

Lynanne grinned, "Wouldn't that be grand?"

There was real concern in Ryan's voice when he asked, "What about your dad? What if he gets caught in the crossfire?"

Susan frowned. "What about us? We could get caught in the same crossfire. I don't know how I feel about *ever* using the phone. And Ryan, you keep talking about Charles as if he were someone else! Do we really want to alert the people who have been looking for you all these years? What if they find you? It sounds like a great plan having the two groups do away with each other, but what if it doesn't happen that way? We have to think this thing through before we do anything."

Ryan had a troubled look on his face. "If we never use the phone, how are we ever going to get out of here?"

Susan was near tears. "I don't know, but I sure don't want them to find you. Charles knew who was chasing him, and he was terrified!"

"Oh."

"Is that all you have to say for yourself, oh?"

Lynanne took over. "Listen, you guys. Whatever we decide to do, you can't contact any organization to come rescue you, and you can't call loved ones back home and tell them you're still alive. You can't get in touch with anyone until we set it up here at the farm."

Ryan looked at Susan's worried face. "Do we have a choice?" he asked her.

"Yes, we have a choice! We have to find a way to survive without using the phone!"

The three sat in silence. With a big sigh of resignation, Ryan crawled out of the fur bed, reached into his jacket pocket, and handed Susan the battery. "Then this is my choice."

"Oh, Ryan! Are you sure? I don't think you completely understand the situation. Charles sure did!"

Ryan stuck out his chin. "I'll just make sure they don't find me."

Lynanne watched Ryan give Susan the battery. Closing her eyes, she prayed. Was that little thing her ticket out of here?

"What exactly could your dad pretend to find that would make the workers think it came from the feds?" Ryan asked.

Lynanne didn't answer. Her eyes were shut, and her lips were moving.

"Lynanne!" Ryan whispered. "Lynanne, Earth calling!"

"Oh!" Lynanne opened her eyes slowly. "I...I...I was praying."

Susan and Ryan looked at each other. It wasn't just the two of them who needed to be rescued. The fifteen-year-old girl added additional incentive for them to come up with a positive plan.

"Ryan, what did you ask me?"

"I was asking if you knew how your dad was going to work his end of this."

"First of all, my dad's name is David."

"Got it. How is David going to work his end of this?"

"Believe me, my dad is really smart. Let's just let him figure that one out."

"How does he feel about our taking you and maybe leaving him behind?"

Lynanne's eyes grew misty. "Dad wants me out of here! We just have to believe that somehow after this is all over, we'll find each other."

That answer made Susan pause and think about her own daughter. The last conversation they had with each other had to have been very upsetting to her. If the cell phone worked from high in the tree, one of the first calls had to be to Julia.

Susan's fingers fumbled in her excitement. "First, let me put in the battery and see if it's working. I won't leave it on long enough for anyone to notice."

The phone sprang to life. For the first time since the crash, there was hope that rescue was possible. Huddled together on the platform, three people sat quietly and thought of what that meant.

Susan's first realization was that her initial desire to get back to her old comfortable but unexciting life wasn't the same; Ryan had changed it. Without any warning, love had broadsided her. The thought of losing him was staggering, but that's what would happen if he regained his memory. Charles hadn't been attracted to her. In fact, he'd been furious with her because she'd asked him if his wife knew about his hidden house and airplane. Was there a wife? And if there was, whatever Laura had done had to be what Charles knew and what Ryan couldn't remember. No, Charles hadn't liked her then, and that was before he lost his house and barn because she'd used her cell phone. Ryan now said he wanted her to use the cell phone again. Should she? If she did, what could happen would be a lot worse than burning down a few buildings. It could end horribly with Ryan's death.

Confusion swirled around in Ryan's mind. Because Lynanne and Susan needed to get out of here, he had made the choice to use the phone. But what if the choice was a bad one? What if he ended up dead? And if he did escape with his life, what kind of world would he be going back to? Was his world still there? And in that world, had he ever felt for another woman the strong feelings that he now had for Susan? The years that were missing from his memory had to contain important events. Was he still married to Laura? There was a memory about her that lurked just outside his grasp. Sometimes he thought he'd glimpsed sight of it, but then a dark force would appear and block it. Why was that? Was it something so awful, so painfully terrible that his brain wouldn't allow him to remember it?

Lynanne sat between her two new friends and thought only positive and happy thoughts. Leaving her dad was going to be painful, but staying here with him was dangerous for both of them. The fact that her dad was smart was a big consolation; if anyone could figure his way out of this, she had to believe it was her dad. She had a future! Now she could let herself dream about school, friends, dances, football games and maybe, just maybe, a boyfriend. Who would she live with once they were rescued? Would either Susan or Ryan take her in? No, it couldn't be Ryan. That poor guy had no idea who he was. Someone was going to have to take him in until he remembered. Would Susan be the answer for both of them?

Ryan broke the silence. "Lynanne, go to the dump and do your thing with the pine cones. We need to talk to David."

CHAPTER 34

Robert Fox was taking his time driving to Ohio; there really wasn't anything to hurry back to. When the police force suspended him, he'd vacated his rented condo, put his furniture into storage, and headed for the easy money in Michigan. Being suspended without pay sucked. How far behind was he in alimony payments to his ex? He didn't even want to think about that one.

Driving off in his buddy's car wasn't the smartest thing he'd ever done. But considering what would have happened to him if Dennis McCain had gotten his hands on him, he had no other choice. Maybe he should just leave the car at the next plaza. And then what? Walk the rest of the way to Ohio?

Pondering his dilemma, he almost missed the notice noise coming from his iPhone; he had an incoming text. Pulling to the side of the road, he stopped, reached behind the seat for his jacket, and fumbled around for his phone.

Dennis McCain's message to Robert was short and to the point. It left nothing to Robert's imagination of what was going to happen to him when, and he assured Robert there would be a when, Dennis caught up with him.

Both fear and rage surged through Robert's body. Having Dennis for an enemy meant a slow but certain death; Dennis never forgot. Feeling the heavy weight of Dennis' threat, he was still sitting with his head in his hands when another phone rang. He had another phone? Fishing around in an inner jacket pocket, he pulled out an unfamiliar phone and answered it. It wasn't until the voice on the other end asked for Julia did he remember. After the call from her mother had been traced on Julia's phone, the phone had been handed back to him.

* * * *

Huddled high in the tree where Lynanne spent the nights, Susan and Ryan cuddled together wrapped in the fur coat. Lynanne had partially crawled into her sleeping bag for warmth.

"Wonder what the temperature really is?" Susan shivered.

Lynanne grinned. "Did you expect central heating in my penthouse?"

A group of workers was gathered close to the tree, excitedly comparing guns.

"Shhhhh!" whispered Ryan. "Whatever your dad told them, it's working!"

The three remained quiet until the group wandered off.

"Looks like the whole camp has been armed so I think it's time we made some calls. Everyone agree?" Susan asked.

Heads nodded.

"Ryan, are you sure? Do you really want to tell the killers where you are?"

Ryan closed his eyes, opened them, and then nodded his head. "Since Charles isn't here to advise me one way or another, I say make the call."

"So, who do we call first?"

"Well, since it's your phone, why don't you call Julia? She must be worried sick about you," Ryan suggested.

"Okay. But we must remember to keep our calls short."

With shaking hands, Susan hit the speed dial key for Julia.

The phone was answered by a male voice.

Puzzled, Susan asked, "Julia?"

The voice that replied had a sneer in it. "Now, really. Do I sound like Julia?"

"No, you don't. Is Julia around? I'd like to speak to her."

"Who's looking for her?"

"I'm her mother."

Susan heard a sudden intake of breath. There was a pause before the voice replied. "Julia's dead."

"D...d...dead?"

"You heard it right, lady. Julia's dead."

The phone dropped out of Susan's hands. Her eyes rolled back, and as she fell against Ryan, Lynanne grabbed the phone and held it to her ear.

"Hello? Are you still there?" she asked.

"Yes, I'm still here, but you aren't Julia's mother."

"She's incapacitated right now. You can talk to me."

"I have an important message for Julia's mother. Listen carefully because I'm going to tell you who killed her. Are you listening?"

"Yes," breathed Lynanne. "I'm listening."

"Dennis McCain killed Julia. Did you hear what I said?"

"Y...y...yes."

"Repeat the message for me."

"Dennis McCain killed Julia."

"You got it right. Now, be sure and tell her mother."

Lynanne didn't have to repeat the message; both Susan and Ryan were staring at her.

Susan went in and out of consciousness. When the grief became too much to bear, she chose to close down. Ryan held her tightly, whispering words of comfort while Lynanne looked on with tears streaming down her face.

＊＊＊＊

Robert grinned, wound down the car's window, and threw Julia's phone into the ditch.

"That should keep Dennis off my back!"

CHAPTER 35

Lynanne waited until Susan's sobs subsided before she pointed to the phone.

"Susan," she said quietly as if she were talking to a gravely ill person, "if you'll give me the area code of your town, I'll call 911 for you..., but when they answer, will you be able to talk to them?"

Susan opened her eyes and sat up. In a flat voice, she said, "There's nothing I can do to bring her back, but I can do something about punishing her killer. The area code is 231. Give me the phone when someone answers."

After repeating her story naming the killer of her murdered daughter three times to three different people, Susan was assured that the police were being notified and that Dennis McCain would be brought in for questioning.

Exhausted from crying, Susan lay quietly in Ryan's arms. For as long as a few seconds at a time she could forget that Julia was dead...and then, with renewed strength, the realization that her daughter was gone would hit her with such force she couldn't breathe.

Unkind thoughts about Charles were running through Ryan's head as he looked down at the devastated woman in his arms. By getting Susan involved in his problem, her daughter had been killed. Ryan tried to feel guilty, but the feeling refused to materialize. How could he feel guilty about something he didn't remember?

Lynanne anxiously watched the two of them, waiting patiently for one of them to take the next step in their plan. It was time to call the Drug Enforcement Agency.

Clearing her throat to get Susan's attention, she said, "If you'll tell me how to reach the DEA's office, I'll make the call, and then you can talk to them, okay?"

Susan roused herself. "Call information and ask them to connect you to the DEA's office, then hand me the phone." Straightening her shoulders, she assured them, "I can do this," she said more to herself than to her companions.

When the office was reached, Susan not only reported the farm's takeover by the growers, she also told them about the organization that would quickly arrive to cash in on a contract placed on a famous golfer who, with a companion, had crashed his plane on the farm. When they asked for the name of the famous golfer, Susan was briefly stumped. Thinking fast, she refused, claiming she was just following the man's wishes. The plan had too many loose ends. The thought of being stuck in the same place as the ones gunning for Ryan was more than scary. It could be deadly.

Their plan to have the two warring groups eliminate each other had to be explained several times. The DEA wasn't sold on the idea, plus there were safety concerns; where were they going to be while this was going on? Susan didn't tell them that she didn't know the answer to that question because they hadn't discussed it. Before she hung up, she said, "...and hold on, I'm going to hand the phone to a person who lives where we crashed. She'll be able to tell you exactly where we are. When this is all over, the golfer and I need to be rescued!"

When Susan turned to give Lynanne the phone, she was surprised to see tears running down her face. "Why, Lynanne! What's wrong?"

"Y...y...you said that just you and the golfer need to be rescued. Does that mean you aren't going to take me with you?"

"Oh, I'm *so* sorry! Yes, I promise, I promise! When we go, you'll be with us! Now would you please tell them where we are so the three of us can get out of here?"

When the call was finished, Susan was worn out. Was there anything more that had to be done? Looking at her phone, she wiped her eyes, straightened her back, and turned to Ryan. "There's still a bar left on my phone. Is there anyone you want to call?"

Ryan thought. "I really don't have any phone numbers in my head...oh, wait. There is one."

"Whose number is it?" asked Lynanne.

Ryan grinned. "Let's call it a mystery number because I have no idea who will answer."

Ryan looked at the cell phone in amazement. Where was the dial? There was nothing to push...just a screen to touch. So much had happened in the ten years that he couldn't remember. Carefully, Ryan's fingers touched the remembered numbers. "Is there any way to put the phone on speaker? I'd like all of us to enjoy my mystery call."

Susan reached over and hit the speaker button just as the phone started to ring. The ringing went on and on. "Bummer. My one number and no one is home!" Ryan complained.

"Maybe there's an answering service. Just wait."

"Hi!" they finally heard. "This is Ted!"

"And this is Laura! We're busy at the moment," she giggled. "You can leave a message or call back in fifteen minutes!"

"Ah, come on Laura! I'm better than that," laughed Ted.

"Well, you tell them how many minutes it's gonna take!" snickered Laura.

"Twenty should do it!"

"You heard the man!" Laura laughed.

Ryan had gotten stone still at the sound of the voices. Fleeting across his face were painful expressions as he remembered times and places. His eyes closed. Slowly, he leaned back...and back...until his head rested on the tree trunk.

Susan and Lynanne looked at each other. "Who's Ted?" asked Lynanne.

"According to Ryan, Ted is his caddy and also his best friend," Susan said with a catch in her voice.

"And Laura?" quizzed Lynanne.

"Laura is Ryan's wife."

Lynanne shook her head. "I don't understand!"

Ryan opened his eyes and uttered two words. "I do."

One look at Ryan and Susan gasped. "You're Charles, aren't you?"

With squinted eyes, Lynanne studied his face. "You look...you look different!"

Ryan shook his head as if to clear it. "Wow!"

Susan looked at him, her eyebrows raised. "Wow? Is that all you have to say for yourself?"

"Yes, wow!" his voice was elated. "We survived the crash!"

Susan's heart had a terrible feeling. Was he going to remember just the things that happened while he was Charles, and remember nothing that had happened while he was Ryan?

"I remember everything," he said quietly, "and I'm so sorry about your daughter. It's my fault that she's dead."

Undone by his words, Susan put her head on his shoulder and sobbed. Expecting that he would put his arms around her, she was surprised to feel his body stiffen.

Lynanne was having a meltdown of her own. While waving the big thick medical book in the air she wailed, "And hearing Ted and Laura's voices brought your memory back? There's nothing like that mentioned in the book!"

Susan didn't respond because Ryan had abruptly stood up. Feeling abandoned, she asked, "Is there something wrong? Are you okay?"

"I feel...I feel as if I just woke up. Is this for real? Or is this a dream?" he threw his hands up in distress. "I remember everything, but it all kind of hazy."

Susan was confused. If he did indeed remember everything, why was he pretending that nothing had happened between them? Memories of what had gone on under the fur coat were making her blush.

Lynanne and Susan watched him as he sat down, looked at the two of them, stood up, and held his head in his hands, and then sat down beside them once again. Leaning his back against the tree trunk, he took a deep breath and began. "Here's my story. My name was never Charles. That was just one of the many aliases that I used while I was running for my life."

"You never said why you were running for your life."

"It's not a pretty story. I exposed a very lucrative and crooked gambling ring."

"Wow! Are you some kind of a hero?" Lynanne asked.

"Hardly! I made an enemy of someone who unfortunately has too much money." Ryan muttered. "Lord, I wish to God I'd kept my mouth shut!"

Lynanne was curious "Ryan, how did it operate?"

"Fixing the outcome of sports games, setting up 'unfortunate' accidents for competitors that several times ended with the death of the player, dirty judges and compliant athletes…you name it. I got involved because, when I was actively playing professional golf, I was one of the athletes they had scheduled to have an unfortunate accident. I figured it out, and ratted on them." He sat silently for a moment and then repeated, "I wish to God I'd kept my mouth shut."

"But you didn't."

"No, I didn't. And I've been running ever since."

"Now that you remember everything, did you make a big mistake when you chose to use the phone?" Susan asked. "They are coming for you, you know."

Ryan shuddered. "I don't know the answer to that, but it doesn't matter; what's done is done."

They sat in silence for a while.

"So your name is really Ryan?" Lynanne asked.

He nodded. "Remember when I told you there was something I needed to remember but I couldn't?"

"I remember. It was something really bad, wasn't it?"

"The worst. Ted, my best friend, turned on me."

"No!" cried Lynanne.

"I was so involved in my good life that I hadn't realized that he had grown to hate me…really hate me." Ryan paused and swallowed hard. "I had the talent and he was just the guy who carried my bag. I made the big bucks, and he had a weekly paycheck. He was also a gambler."

Ryan stopped talking. Betrayal, although it had happened years ago, still hurt.

"Ted not only hated me, he was also in over his head in gambling debts, so when he was contacted by the organization that had the contract on me and was offered a lot of money, he jumped at the chance."

"How awful!" cried Lynanne.

"That's not the worst part," Ryan said quietly.

Lynanne looked unconvinced. "How can something be more horrible than that?"

Taking a deep breath, he looked at Susan who hadn't said a word during his explanation. Should he go on with the embarrassing story? If his own wife hadn't been able to love him, what did that say about him? What kind of a man was he that his best friend had no qualms about betraying him? As if being rejected by the two most important people in his life wasn't bad enough, there was also that damned contract hanging over his head. How could he ever get involved with a woman? His amnesia had allowed him to fall in love with Susan, and oh, how he had fallen. It was as if he had waited his whole life to find her, and now that he had found her, he couldn't have her. He closed his eyes and willed his heart to move the love to a corner and cement a wall around it. Susan was going to be hurt, but not as badly as she would have been if they'd remained together.

Opening his eyes, he finished the story. "Ted and my wife had been having an affair."

No one said a word while waiting for Ryan to regain his composure.

"When Laura saw there was a way to get rid of me plus have a share in the money, she and Ted disappeared. But not entirely."

Susan squeezed his hand. "What do you mean, not entirely?"

Ryan pulled his hand away. "I'd forgotten that Laura's name was on one of my accounts where I had banked a large sum of money. Laura and Ted watched that one source and followed it whenever I withdrew money from the account. They shared that information with the organization. That's the way I was found several times."

"But Ryan!" Susan jumped into the conversation. "That number you called must have been your old phone number! What are Ted and Laura doing in your house?"

"After seven years, Laura had me declared legally dead even though she knew that I wasn't. Ted's gambling debts were huge. They used the money from my life insurance policy to pay them off. She inherited the house and most of my money. But when she didn't lay her hands on the one account, that's when I realized that her name was on it and that's how they were tracking me."

"So, what have you been living on?"

"I still have some off-shore accounts that she doesn't know about."

For the longest time, the three sat quietly high in the tree, mulling over his explanation. Breaking the silence, Susan asked, "Have you ever thought about what you would do if you could get the contract removed?"

"I can't see that happening. The kingpin is still in prison pulling all the strings. If the workers kill all the contract people that invade this area trying to find me, the guy in prison will just hire more."

"So, your only out would be if the guy in prison runs out of money or dies?"

"That about the size of it."

In sympathy, Susan reached out to touch Ryan; he moved away and stood up.

The rest of the day passed in a strained silence. After a few more attempts to find out what was going on with Ryan, Susan gave up.

She swallowed the last bitter pill when, as darkness fell, he exclaimed, "You girls can sleep up here tonight. I'll sleep on the lower platform."

Lynanne and Susan watched Ryan crawl down the tree.

"What's going on between you two?" Lynanne whispered.

Susan wiped away a tear that was working its way down her cheek. "Charles never liked me."

"But Ryan did!" Lynanne whispered back. "He *really* liked you!"

Susan nodded. Her heart ached. To be awakened from the long empty years by the thrill of love had been intoxicating. How could a feeling so newly created leave such a devastating wound when it was lost? The open sore inside her heart was deep and wide.

Pulling the heavy coat around her, she closed her eyes and tried to sleep. Hours later, still awake, she threw off the coat and sat up. Lynanne was sleeping soundly, and lower in the tree she could hear Ryan muttering in his sleep. Without the coat, he was probably cold; Susan felt no sympathy for him.

What do you do at night in a treehouse when you can't sleep? Reaching into her jacket pocket, she pulled out her cell phone. If only she had a charger, she could play games while waiting for dawn. As it was, there was very little remaining of the last bar. Surprised at the amount of light it threw in the total blackness of the night, she quickly dove back under the coat. While scrolling through her contacts, the word 'home' brought tears to her eyes. One touch of the screen and she'd be connected to the phone on her desk. Would she ever sit at that desk again? It surprised her how much she wanted to do that. For a quiet minute, she sat and looked at her cell, and then, with loving fingers, she touched the well-remembered number. Closing her eyes, she pictured her house, her den, and the desk that the phone was setting on. She'd just let it ring once or twice, and then she'd hang up.

The ringing was music to her ears, but enough was enough. She was about to end the call when a female voice answered.

"Hello?"

CHAPTER 36

If a lake lot that sold for $750.00 a foot, and the lot was 132 feet deep with an area of 7,568 square feet, how much did the lot sell for?

Grinning, Denny waved the calculator in the air and congratulated himself for coming up with the right answer to the question.

After finding Susan's calculator and samples of the real estate test in a desk drawer, he'd spent hours plowing through the questions. What were the chances that he'd still have a teaching job after this was all over? Selling houses had to be better than flipping hamburgers.

Moving on, he was working on Molly's problem. She wanted to buy a cottage costing $150,000.00 and she needed a 10% down payment and she had to pay a 1% origination fee, 2 points discount and a 0.5% PMI. How much money did she need....

The sound of a car starting next door interrupted his attempt at solving Molly's problem. Standing to the side of the window, he watched Joe and Judy Binder backing out of the driveway. It was unusual for both of them to leave the house at the same time. Ever since they'd hidden Julia, one of them always remained in the house with her.

Denny shrugged; he was sure they had a good reason. He was about to go back and solve Molly's problem, when he saw the side door open at the Binders' house. Since there was no one but the Binders and Julia in that house, and the Binders had just driven away, that meant....

He mouthed, "No, no, Julia! Don't."

In a matter of seconds, Julia had arrived at her mother's house. Frightened that someone might see her, she was frantically pounding on the door when Denny opened it and roughly pulled her into the house.

"Are you trying to get yourself killed?" he barked.

"For God's sake, Denny!" complained Julia as she pushed him away. "I'm scared enough without you adding to it!"

"What if someone had seen you?"

"Come on, Denny. I'm bored to death!"

Denny reached out and squeezed her arm. "Believe me, being bored to death is better than actually being dead!" he grinned. "You're here, so let's drop the argument."

Her eyes landed on the cluttered work area on the desk. "You found something to occupy your time?"

"Your mother has a number of books on real estate. I read them all before I found her calculator along with samples of the exam you have to pass to get a license."

Julia wrinkled her nose. "I remember Mom doing those samples. What surprised me were the words she muttered when she couldn't figure out the right answer." Realizing what she had just said, tears gathered in her eyes. "I...I...I keep forgetting...."

When Denny stepped forward with his arms open, Julia walked into them. He wasted only a few seconds of the incredulous moment to have a fleeting pang of guilt for taking advantage of her. Holding her tightly, his heart raced as he soothed the sobbing girl.

Julia gave one last hiccup, dropped her arms, and stepped away. "Will you forgive me for getting your collar wet with my tears?" she asked.

"Wh...what?" he stammered. How could she want to talk about his tear-soaked collar?

"Your collar...it's all wet."

With a sinking feeling, Denny realized she hadn't felt the electricity of the hug.

"My collar? Ah, no problem." He couldn't believe that Julia was acting as if nothing important had happened.

"Aren't you curious why I risked everything to sneak over here?"

"You already said you were bored. Is there another reason?" Denny's heart skipped a beat. Was she going to say she risked everything just to be with him?

"I need something to read," Julia said casually as she breezed past him on the way to Susan's den. "Mom has a lot of paperbacks. She always kept one in her purse to read at Sunday open houses. Lots of times no one shows up."

Julia had piled up several books on the desk and was looking for more when the phone rang. It was just the most natural thing in the world for Julia to reach out and answer it.

"Hello?"

Denny tried to grab the phone out of her hand. "Julia, hang up! You can't answer the phone!"

From the receiving end of the phone, they both heard a female voice cry, "Julia?"

"Mom?" Julia yelled.

And the phone went dead.

CHAPTER 37

"Julia, Julia," Susan screamed into the dead phone.

Lynanne stuck her head out of the sleeping bag. "For God's sake, Susan! Are you trying to get us all killed?"

"Julia! She's not dead! I just talked to her!" Susan shouted.

Ryan's head appeared at the top of their platform. "What's going on?"

Lynanne gestured for Ryan to join them. "Please, can you get her to quiet down?"

Ryan crawled onto their platform and slid his body to where Susan was laughing and crying between shouts of, "She's not dead!"

"Shhhh! Susan!" he whispered. "You have to cut this out! Just quiet down and tell us what's going on."

Breathing hard, Susan held up her cell phone. "I called…just wanted to…and Julia…and Julia…it was Julia who answered the phone! I swear I heard her voice!"

Ryan's arms were outstretched, ready to gather Susan in his arms, when he remembered; he dropped his arms. "Susan," he whispered. "You're having a dream!"

"It wasn't a dream! Julia isn't dead!" she yelled.

"That's what we'll all be if you can't get her to shut up!" hissed Lynanne to Ryan.

"Shhhh! Susan!" Ryan pleaded.

"Are you listening to m...." Susan's cry was shut off. Ryan had placed his hand over her mouth.

She bit him.

"Ouch!" he cried.

"Not you, too!" whined Lynanne.

In the distance, the sound of a motor starting up silenced them all.

"Oh, now you've gone and done it." Lynanne was near tears. "We're all going to die!"

Out of the dark, a large tractor was speeding toward them.

"If we're lucky, that's Dad. If it's not, we're dead!"

When the tractor stopped under the tree, Lynanne's dad whispered hoarsely, "I'll say this just once. I'm counting to ten and then I'm driving off. I have room for all three of you if you can make it down the tree in time. They're right behind me. Oh, bring your sleeping gear. One, two, three, four, five, six, seven, eight, nine,...."

By the count of ten, the tractor drove away with two bodies hidden under garbage bags.

"Dad! Wait! Susan didn't make it!"

David didn't say a word.

"Ryan, make Dad stop!"

"I'm not stopping." David's voice was muffled by the noise of the tractor's motor. "They're right behind us!"

Peeking out between bags, they saw workers with flashlights milling around in the vicinity of their tree.

"Ryan, how could you leave Susan behind?"

"I...I...I thought she was right behind me!"

"Really? The way you've been treating her, I think you might have held her back on purpose."

"How can you say something like that?"

"Because you've turned into a real shithead," Lynanne hissed.

"Quiet back there!" ordered David. "My life is on the line right now. You get me into trouble and we're all dead! I'm supposed to be out looking for the noisemakers. What the hell were you thinking?"

"It was Susan, Dad. We couldn't get her to stop!"

"She bit me!" complained Ryan.

Lynanne scoffed. "Baby!"

David asked in a stern whisper, "What was so important that she'd risk my daughter's life? I've kept you safe for over a year and then she pulls a stunt like this!"

"Dad, tell me this. If someone had told you that I was dead, and then the phone rang and I was on the other end of the call, what do you think you would do?"

"Probably yell." David thought a bit, and then he asked. "Is that what happened?"

Ryan sneered. "Nothing happened like that. Susan just had a dream…in this case, a good dream, but that's what it was."

"It was no dream!"

Ryan confronted Lynanne. "Did Julia call Susan? I sure didn't hear her phone ring."

Lynanne flinched. Oh, how she missed the old Ryan! She was clutching the rolled sleeping bag, and Ryan was shivering in one of David's old jackets. By now, the tractor had covered some distance from the tree.

Lynanne broke the silence. "What are we going to do about Susan?"

"Nothing. Honey, you were on your own for over a year. Surely Susan can hide until this blows over. If she doesn't make any more noise, the workers will have nothing to go on and they'll go back to the house."

The tractor stopped. "I'm going to leave you here. The stream is quite close so you'll have water. One of the bags back there has a bit of food in it…I didn't have time to put much in it, though. There's been a lot of chatter about the DEA, and I suppose you've noticed that all the workers are armed. I'd like for you to be out of the combat area before all hell breaks loose. So just keep walking away from the farm."

"So you're leaving us? Susan is back there all alone, and you're leaving us?"

Ryan turned his head. Lynanne didn't need to see the tears running down his face. "Susan, Susan," he cried to himself. "How did this happen?"

David was thinking like a father. Could he really drive away and leave his attractive teenager alone with a complete stranger? What did he know about Ryan? Absolutely nothing. But when he saw the man trying to brush away the tears that were running down his face, he relaxed. Ryan obviously had feeling for the absent Susan. "I'm going back. They'll be looking for me."

"But Dad!" cried Lynanne. "You don't even have a gun! You'll get killed if you go back there!"

"Lynanne, honey, you stay with your friend. He's the best bet you have of getting away from the farm. I don't have a choice…I have to go back." With that, he threw a plastic bag at their feet, started the tractor, and drove away into the night.

* * * *

Susan's heart was in her mouth. With a sinking feeling, she watched the tractor pulling away without her. How could they leave her behind? Damn coat! It was the coat's fault she'd missed the ride to safety. Hurrying down the tree after Ryan, the coat had gotten hung up on a branch, and by the time she'd jerked it free, David had counted to ten.

Men with flashlights were milling around, muttering to themselves as they flashed their lights around the base of the trees and occasionally up into them. Susan froze. Slowly she spread the brown coat over her body trying her best to blend in with the bark of the tree. When the lights moved on, she felt her way, branch by branch past the first platform, and up to the higher one where Lynanne spent the nights.

Thinking the danger was past, she figured all she had to do was keep out of sight until daylight when, she was sure, the others would come back.

She could do this. After all, how hard could it be? Lynanne had been on her own for over a year.

Wrapped in the coat, her descent into sleep was rudely interrupted by the sound of a gunshot. The reply to the one blast was horrendous. From her lofty perch, she watched armed men coming from two different directions shooting randomly at anything that moved. Bullets were flying, and bodies were falling.

She watched in horror as one man, running while looking over his shoulder, collided with her tree. Foreign-sounding words poured out of the man's mouth that, even though she couldn't understand what he was saying, she figured he was just venting his deep displeasure at the tree for getting in his way. When the battle moved away from her area, she gave a sigh of relief. If the worse thing that had happened to her in the middle of the gunfight was a man running into her tree, then she was lucky.

Wait a minute. What was that noise? It sounded…it sounded like someone breathing. Deep breathing. Was someone climbing her tree?

The face of a man appeared at the edge of her platform. Susan swallowed a scream as the man, a knife clenched between his teeth, had one leg up, ready to swing it over the edge.

With strength she didn't know she possessed, Susan gave his body a mighty push. His cry of surprise, anger, and fear followed him to his death when he hit the ground.

Susan hung her head over the platform and vomited.

CHAPTER 38

"Mom?" Julia yelled. "Mom, don't hang up! Mom?"

Denny watched as the happy expression on Julia's face turned into one of despair. With a cry of anguish, she collapsed. Denny caught her before she hit the floor.

When her eyes opened, the first thing she saw was Denny's concerned face. He has such nice brown eyes! Should she tell him that she had dreams about those eyes?

"Julia! Thank God you're awake! What was that phone call about?"

The phone call…the phone call… Julia's face lit up. "Mom's not dead! She's not dead, Denny!"

"That was your mom on the phone?" Denny was uneasy. Was Julia imagining things?

"Yes! It was Mom! She said, 'Julia?' and I said 'Mom?', and then the phone went dead." Julia burst into tears. "Mom's alive!" she sobbed. "Oh, thank you, God! Mom's not dead!"

Denny held her close. "Are you sure?"

Julia wiped her wet face on her sleeve. "We can check."

With his help, Susan got to her feet. Picking up the phone, she pressed 'menu' and then clicked on 'recent calls'. She pointed to the displayed number. "See? That's Mom's cell number!"

If Julia said that was Susan's number, he'd have to take her word for it. "What did she tell you in the last conversation you had with her?"

Julia closed her eyes and remembered. "I was on the floor of Robert Fox's police car when I had my last conversation with Mom."

Denny looked at her closely. Where was this story coming from?

Julia saw his puzzled look. "Oh, haven't I told you about that?"

"No, and I really think you should."

She started the story on the day she came home and learned that her neighbor had been snatched, and ended it with her thinking that she'd found safety in the blue-eyed cop's car; that's when her mom called.

"Wow!" was all wide-eyed Denny could think to say. "So we're back to your mom's call. What did she say?"

"It was about her Pittsburgh buyer. He was in some kind of trouble and somehow he got Mom mixed up in it. He'd taken the battery out of her phone so she couldn't call anyone. When he went outside without his jacket to start his plane, she put the battery back in and called me."

"Start a plane? Your mom flew off with her buyer?"

"I guess so. But then Robert Fox grabbed the phone out of my hand and when I fought to get it back, he knocked me out."

Denny flinched. "Where did he take you?"

"You know...the house where you rescued me. Oh, that's where I heard that Mom's phone call had been traced and the hit men were going there to do away with both of them. One of the cops was wondering if there was money in the contract to collect on the death of the real estate lady." Julia paused to regain her composure. "That's how I found out that Mom was dead."

Denny grinned. "Apparently not!"

"But if she's not dead, where is she?"

"Hiding?"

The sound of a car pulling into Binders' driveway silenced them.

"It can't be Joe and Judy!" Julia wailed. "They went to a two hour show at the mall!"

Standing sideways at the edge of the window, Denny saw his dad walk up to the Binders' door. "Julia, come here," he hissed.

They watched as Dennis swiped something along the edge of the door, then turned the doorknob and walked in.

Julia was having trouble breathing. "Oh, Denny! Wh…what if I hadn't come over here? That man…."

"But you did!" Denny put his arms around her. When she didn't object, he pulled her closer.

Julia pulled back and looked into Denny's face. "What did he do with that thing he swiped down the door?"

"That was probably a credit card. It never works when I try to open a locked door that way but Dad seems to know how to do it."

"But he didn't need a credit card to open the door!" Julia exclaimed. "The door wasn't locked!"

＊＊＊＊

Dennis had been driving around Susan Cook's neighborhood for hours. He was certain both his son and Julia were in one of the houses, but which one? With luck and persistence, he was sure he'd get a glimpse of one of them; it was just a matter of time.

In his mind he kept going over the visit he'd paid to the idiots that lived next door to Susan. How could two people that dumb ever find each other? The more he thought about it, the more their story sounded phony. But was it false enough to follow up with another visit? Probably not.

About to give up for the day, he was surprised to see a car with both idiots in it heading in the direction of town.

With a satisfied grin on his face, he drove back to the Binder house.

Getting in was easy…if people only knew how easy it was, they'd get better locks put on their doors. When a quick check of the empty house didn't produce either his son or Julia, he left by the same door that he'd gone in. He even put the lock back on so the idiots would never know that anyone had been in their house.

Standing outside the Binders' door, he paused, looked over at Susan's house, and wondered once again if he should check her house, too. It was a tempting thought, but again he came to the conclusion that even his dumbhead son wouldn't be stupid enough to hide there.

With one last look at her house, he turned to walk to his car…and then stopped. Why not check it out? He was here, and even though her house looked empty, he needed to be sure.

With the credit card in his hand, he was preparing to unlock the front door of Susan's house when his cell phone rang.

"Hello?"

"Dennis?"

"Yeah. Who is this?"

"Lloyd."

"Why didn't you say so?"

"Well, I'm saying so."

"And you're calling about…?"

Lloyd cleared his throat. "Uh, it's kinda like the police were here looking for you."

"What?"

"I said, th…"

"I heard you the first time! Why are they looking for me?"

"Uh, they think you killed Julia."

"What?"

"Uh, they th…"

"I heard you the first time!"

"Then quit saying what!"

Dennis sputtered. "Why do the police think I killed Julia?"

"Because her mother called them."

"Her mother?"

"Yeah, her mother. Seems someone using Julia's cell phone told her that Dennis McCain killed her daughter."

"Well, you and I know that Julia isn't dead. Did you tell the police that?"

"I didn't tell the police nothing."

"What am I supposed to do?"

"If you don't want them finding you and hauling you off to the station for questioning, I'd suggest you turn yourself in."

Dennis thought for a minute. "Know what? That's a good idea. I'll go to the police station and tell them that they're looking for the wrong Dennis McCain."

"Come on! Are you saying that there's another one of you?"

"I don't think I've ever told you the name of my son."

Lloyd was laughing when Dennis ended the call.

About to head for his car, he turned back to the door when he realized he was still holding the credit card. It would only take a couple of minutes to go through Susan's house, and since he was already here, he might as well do it. But wait a minute. If the police were looking for him, maybe he should go to the station before they found him. He didn't need the embarrassment of having them haul him to the station. Anyhow, he was eager to tell them that they were looking for the wrong Dennis McCain. He couldn't find Denny, but he was betting that the police could.

* * * *

Huddled together inside Susan's house, Julia and Denny watched in horror as Dennis turned around and headed in their direction.

"Where can we hide?" Julia panted. The memory of being tied up while waiting for someone to kill her was still raw.

Before Denny had a chance to answer, they heard the faint sound of a cell phone's ring. Dennis was standing right outside the front door when he answered it.

Julia was terrified. The man who had given the order for her death was right outside the door. "Denny, let's get out of here!"

Denny's legs didn't want to move. Wild thoughts were racing through his head. That was his dad out there. *His dad!* Until a few days ago, he'd thought Dennis was like everyone's dad, albeit a cold one, but certainly not an evil one. The crushing realization that his own dad would have no compunction qualms about killing him, his own son, was devastating.

Julia pulled his arm. "For God's sake, Denny! Don't just stand there!"

Denny was trying to shake off the disgust that he was feeling when he became aware that he could hear most of what his dad was saying.

"Wait...wait! Listen!"

When the call ended, they watched Dennis turn as if to go back to his car.

With a shudder, Julia murmured, "Thank you, God."

Almost as an afterthought, Dennis turned. With the credit card in his hand, he looked at the door, looked at the credit card, and then looked back at the door again.

Julia grabbed Denny's hand and squeezed.

When Dennis shrugged, put the card back into his pocket and walked away, the two collapsed into each other's arms.

"Whew!" Denny blew out the breath he'd been holding. "That was close!"

Julia's body didn't stop shaking until she saw Dennis back out of the driveway...then she burst into tears.

Denny held her close. "He's gone."

"I...I was...so scared!" Julia managed to get out before the sobs turned to hiccups.

Holding on to each other, the two stood in the middle of the room recovering from the terrifyingly close call. Finally, when Julia's sobs and hiccups had subsided, she dried her face on her sleeve, looked up at Denny, and with a puzzled look on her face, asked, "Did I hear right? Did he say that my mother called the police with the information that Dennis McCain had killed me?"

"Since we could only hear one end of the conversation, that's what it sounded like."

"Can you remember the exact word of the conversation?"

"Uh, we heard Dad say 'Why do they think I killed Julia?'. We couldn't hear what the person on the other end said, but Dad's surprised reaction was, 'Her mother?'"

"But why would my mother think that I was dead?"

Denny shrugged. "The caller might have told Dad, but he didn't repeat it."

"But if she made the phone call, that's more proof that Mom's alive, right?"

Denny didn't reply. He was still struggling with the fact that his dad was so blatantly evil.

"Mom's alive!" Julia clapped her hands. "Mom's ali...." One look at Denny's somber face and Julie cut short her celebration. "Are you thinking bad thoughts about your dad?"

Denny's face relaxed. "You got me!"

Julia put her arms around him. "And for good reasons! I heard what your dad said!"

"That's my dad! Wasn't that a nice fatherly thing for him to do?" There was both pain and loathing in Denny's voice.

"Even though he knows I'm alive, your own dad is going to tell the police that you are the one they should be looking for."

Denny nodded. "I'm not surprised. There's never been any love between us. It used to bother me a lot."

Julia looked puzzled. "Are you saying that it doesn't bother you anymore?"

"I tried for years to please that man, but I finally gave up. I don't even try anymore."

Julia just shook her head. With a dad like that, it was a miracle that Denny had turned into such a nice guy.

Denny broke into her thoughts. "Since we're pretty sure my dad is at the police station, I think it's safe for you to go back."

Julia nodded, gave Denny a hug, and left.

Denny watched her race out of the house, and when she got to the door, she turned and waved; she'd made it back safely. He was about to return to his real estate problem and help Molly buy her cottage when he saw Julia running back toward him.

He met her at the door before she had a chance to pound on it.

"What's going on?"

"I'm locked out!" she wailed.

CHAPTER 39

The sun was sliding to the west when Ryan, who was carrying the bag that David had thrown to them, stopped walking. "We should start looking for a place to spend the night."

Lynanne dropped the bulky sleeping bag. "I'm really thirsty! Did Dad put anything to drink in the bag?"

"Lynanne, Lynanne! Always complaining," he mocked. "You must have been one hell of a Girl Scout!"

"Ryan, you're acting like a shithead again!"

With a smirk on his face, he threw up his hands. "Guilty!"

"Well, cut it out! But you didn't answer my question. Did Dad put anything to drink in the bag?"

"Let's look," Ryan said.

There was very little in the bag. No one said a word as Ryan pulled the few things out and lined them up.

In an effort to make an excuse for her dad, Lynanne casually mentioned, "Dad did say that he didn't have time to grab a lot of food for us."

"That could be the understatement of the year," Ryan muttered. "And the answer to your question is no. Your dad didn't put anything to drink in the bag, but he did say the stream was close by."

"The woods are so thick you really can't tell one direction from another. Wonder how far we've walked?"

Ryan grinned.

"You know something funny? You're grinning."

"It happened before we met you. I'm remembering when Susan and I ran and ran, thinking we were going away from the workers who were looking to kill anyone who'd survived the plane crash."

"So?" Lynanne asked.

"Turns out, we were running in a circle."

"No!" laughed Lynanne.

"Yes," chuckled Ryan. "We ended up right back where we started."

Lynanne stopped walking. Holding up a finger for silence, she cocked her head. "Oh, my! I think you did it again!"

"Did what again?"

"Can't you hear it?"

"Hear what?"

An airplane coming in for a landing flew low over their heads.

"That!" Lynanne pointed to the sky. "The airport is near the farm."

"But...but...," stammered Ryan. "I thought I was leading us away from the farm!"

"Ryan, Ryan," mocked Lynanne. "You must have been one hell of a Boy Scout!"

Ryan gave her a dirty look.

"Aw, come on, Ryan. You have to admit that you deserved tha....."

A sudden burst of ground gunfire erupted close to where they were standing. Lynanne's face turned white. "My God! We're in the middle of the fighting!"

A tractor crashing through the underbrush cut off her comment. The surprised look on her dad's face turned into one of terror as a burst of machine gun fire shot off the bark of a nearby tree.

"Girl, what the hell are you doing here?" he yelled. "You were supposed to be far away by this time!"

Ryan stammered. "I…you know…uh…well…."

"Translated," Lynanne broke in, "he's saying that he has a lousy sense of direction."

Fear for his daughter put anger into his voice. "Your lousy sense of direction is going to get you both killed!"

Wanting to get the attention off him, Ryan asked, "What's going on back there?"

"They're killing each other!" David almost grinned. "Without uniforms to identify what side they're on, they're just shooting anything that moves…especially the ones here to do away with you. A lot of them had never seen each other before they got here."

Ryan's face turned white.

"Has the Drug Enforcement Agency shown up?" Lynanne asked.

"Not that I'm aware of, but I did have a bit of a scare back there," David said, pointing to the way he had come. "There's a guy back there shooting like there's no tomorrow, and it's the strangest thing…." David's voice tapered off.

"Finish it, Dad! What's the strangest thing?"

David's eyes landed on Ryan. "Ryan, do you have a twin?"

Ryan froze. "You saw someone back there that looks just like me. Right?"

"No," David shook his head. "Strange. His face didn't look like yours, but the rest of him did."

"Ted?" whispered Lynanne. Of course Ted's face would be different from Ryan's. He hadn't had all the plastic surgery that had changed Ryan's face. With a cry of anguish, Ryan turned his back; his shoulders were shaking.

David's eyes questioned his daughter. When she didn't say a word, he asked, "Is someone gonna tell me who this Ted guy is?"

Lynanne was watching Ryan trying to control his emotions. "Ted? He's a guy who's related to Ryan. He also used to be his best friend."

David snorted. "Best friend, my foot! I heard him offering a bonus for anyone who could bring the golfer to him."

Ryan whirled around. "He wants me alive?"

"Guess so." David winced as a nearby gun went off. "No more talking! Jump on...we need to go rescue your friend."

* * * *

Exhausted, Susan huddled inside the coat and tried to close her eyes. If she lived to be a hundred, she'd never forget the face that had appeared at the edge of the platform. Pushing the man to his death had taken its toll on her. She had gone through phases of weeping, shivering, and praying. When she doubted that she could have done such a thing, one glance at the crumpled body at the bottom of the tree convinced her that indeed she had done such a thing.

She was semiconscious when a sound pulled her out of her stupor. The first thing she saw was a face peering at her from the edge of the platform.

Susan screamed and passed out.

Startled, Ryan jerked back and lost his balance. When one of his flailing arms came in contact with a branch, he grabbed it and held on for dear life. He was breathing hard by the time he regained his footing; he didn't look down at the ground.

When he was safely back on the platform, he did something he'd been longing to do. Realizing that this might be his last chance, he tenderly gathered her still body into his arms, hugged her, cherished her, buried his nose in her hair, and inhaled her essence. "Susan, my love," he whispered. He held her until he heard the noisy approach of Lynanne who was climbing up to them. Laying Susan back down, he kissed her one last time and yelled, "There's something wrong with Susan!"

Lynanne was hovered over Susan lamenting the fact that she had no water to put on Susan's forehead to wake her, when Susan's eyes opened.

With a jerk, she sat up.

"Oh, my God! It's you!"

Ryan asked gruffly, "Well, who in the hell did you think it would be?"

Susan burst into tears.

David called up from the base of the tree. "Everything okay up there?"

Susan had to tell and retell her story, hugs and tears had been freely shared, and David was not only getting impatient, he was also rolling his eyes. Someone had removed the body, the only proof that her story was true.

When Susan shifted the heavy coat from one arm to the other, Ryan asked, "The coat getting too heavy for you?"

Susan shrugged. "It was the coat getting caught on a branch that slowed me down and you guys left me behind."

"Well, since I'm going to be using it tonight, maybe I'm the one who should be carrying it."

Susan blinked back tears. Oh, how she missed the old Ryan! Tossing the coat at him, she replied coldly, "You want the coat? Take it."

Ryan bit his tongue. What he wanted right now, more than food or drink, was to be with Susan inside the coat; his arms felt so empty they ached. But he had said it, and he couldn't take it back. He stooped and picked it up.

Lynanne caught Susan's eye. "Don't worry," she mouthed. "I'll share my sleeping bag with you."

Susan nodded. "Thanks," she mouthed back.

David drove them as far as he figured he could go before his leg alarm would go off, and knowing they would need water, he left them by the stream. After pointing out that even though the woods were thick and the view of the sky was obstructed, the way away from the farm was mostly uphill. Before he drove away, he reminded them that if they ever felt as if they were walking downhill, they were going in the wrong direction.

Ryan had a troubled look on his face as he watched him disappear. "I wonder if he'll run into Ted again." Just saying Ted's name made goosebumps run up and down both his arms.

Susan whirled around. "David saw Ted? He's here?"

Ryan shrugged. "Wasn't that the plan?"

"Oh my God!" Susan breathed. "What do we do now?"

"There're acres of woods for us to hide in. We have no weapons so distance is our best bet. Let's get as far away from the farm as we can before it gets too dark."

Ryan turned his back on Susan to hide the fact that his whole body was shaking. The gang that he'd been running from for the past ten years was here. David had said that Ted wanted him alive. For what? The contract, to his knowledge, was just to kill him. Why did Ted want him alive? Another reason to turn his back on Susan was to escape her eyes. There was love, concern, and hurt in those eyes. He was strong in his conviction that he couldn't have her, but how wonderful it would be to give in and just love her.

He shook himself back to reality when he heard Lynanne saying, "I wish Dad wasn't going back."

"It is his farm," he reminded her. "I suppose he wants to be there after the DEA gets the workers out of the house and off his land."

"But he's driving right into the fighting and he doesn't even have a gun!" Lynanne wailed.

Susan put her arms around the girl. There was no sense in saying that everything was going to be okay, because there was a good chance that everything was *not* going to be okay. They stood with their arms entwined until Lynanne raised her head. "Did I just feel a drop of rain?"

It took some time before the rain made it through the trees, but when it did, they huddled together under the thickest tree they could find. Darkness was coming fast. After a meal of plenty of water but little food, Ryan took the coat and laid it down on damp moss that was around the base of the tree. Lynanne and Susan unrolled the sleeping bag.

"How do you figure we do this?" Susan asked.

"I guess we won't know until we try. Wanna be first in?"

"Okay," Susan agreed as she crawled into the bag. "There doesn't seem to be much room for another body in here."

"Are you back as far as you can go?" Lynanne asked. "I don't think this is going to work. I'm getting really wet!"

Ryan, snug in the big coat that he'd pulled over his head, was listening. What he wanted to say, he couldn't say. Susan should be here beside him warm and dry inside the coat, but she wasn't, and she'd never be… ever again. It surprised and scared him how strong his feelings for her had grown in such a short period of time. How comforting it would be to have her here. Ted, who used to be his best friend, was out there some place close hunting him down like a dog, and he had pushed Susan, the one person he loved, away. By handing Susan the cell battery, he had probably signed his own death warrant. Just when he'd found the person he wanted to spend the rest of his life with. He shook his head to chase away the thoughts. Nothing could be done about it now.

He could hear the two of them giggling while crawling over each other trying to find a dry spot in a sleeping bag that was too small for both of them.

"Okay, girls! I give up!" he called out. "I'll trade you my fur bed for your wet sleeping bag. Deal?"

By now, the rain was coming down hard. The trade was made with much giggling and squealing from getting soaked by the cold rain, and much shivering and shaking from the drop in temperature. The two women quickly settled down in their warm nest and went to sleep. Ryan wasn't that lucky. When sleep finally came to him, it brought along dreams; unfortunately, not good ones.

CHAPTER 40

"You're locked out?" Denny asked. "How did that happen?"

Julia was breathing hard. "I don't know! I was very, very careful to make sure the door was unlocked before I ran over here. I don't want the Binders to find out that I put them in danger just because I wanted a book to read!"

"You forgot the books, anyhow. They're back in your mom's den by the phone."

"Forget about the books! How am I going to get back into the house before they get home?"

Denny scratched his head. "So when Dad thought he'd unlocked the door by swiping his credit card, it wasn't locked?"

"What do you think happened?"

"Dad must have thought he was being a good citizen by locking the door on his way out."

Julia made a face. "Your dad a good citizen? I don't think so!"

Denny looked over at the house. "Do you think they might have a hidden key somewhere?"

"It wouldn't hurt to look...and do you have a credit card?"

"Yes I do but I've never been able to unlock a door with one."

"Bummer!" Julia exclaimed. "That would have been such an easy solution. But I do want those books, so I'll just run inside and grab them. Be right back!"

Denny was waiting for Julia to reappear when the sound of a slow-moving vehicle caught his ear. Still on edge from the close call he had just lived through, he ducked behind a low bush by the door's entrance. When the car stopped for a moment by the driveway, he could easily see the man behind the wheel. It was his dad.

The car moved on. Denny stayed behind the bush and listened to the sound of the car turning around in a neighbor's driveway.

Fear gave speed to his feet as he jumped from behind the bush and into the house before the car came back in sight.

"What the…!" Julia yelled. The books fell out of her arms and onto the floor.

"Don't ask questions, just run out the back door! Dad is about to pull into the driveway."

"No!" squealed Julia.

"Yes!" Denny shouted. "Go!"

Huddled together, they waited until Dennis got out of his car and when he walked to a spot where a tree would keep them out of his dad's sight, they raced to the tool shed in the back of Susan's property. Dennis stood for a few moments outside the house, and then, as if he'd made a decision, he nodded his head, reached into his pocket for the credit card, and walked up to the front door.

"The door's not locked!" Denny whispered.

Once again, Dennis thinking he'd done magic with the card, smiled and opened the door. The next thing they heard was a thump and some swear words.

Julia caught her breath. "I think he just fell over my books!"

Within minutes, Dennis walked out of the house and back to his car. They stayed behind the shed until they could no longer hear the engine.

"Whooo!" Denny breathed.

"My heart can't take much more of this!" Julia gasped.

"Well, he's gone. Let's get your books and then go next door. Maybe we'll find a window that we can open from the outside."

With his hand on the doorknob of Susan's front door, Denny smiled down at Julia as he turned it. His smile vanished when the knob didn't turn.

* * * *

Dennis gave up. It had been a good theory and he had to play it to its end, but now he was satisfied that if Julia and his son were living somewhere in the neighborhood, it wasn't in the two houses that he'd checked. He'd failed in his search, but the day wasn't a complete washout; he'd opened two locked doors with a credit card.

The visit to the police station had been an easy one. Since there was no body, all the police had was a call from a woman claiming to be Julia's mother accusing Dennis McCain of murdering her daughter. After he explained that Julia and Dennis Junior taught at the same school while he, Dennis Senior, had never met the girl, it had been quite easy to shift the blame from him to his son..., and no, he had no idea where Dennis Junior was.

So now, he would just sit back and let the police find Denny.

* * * *

"How does he do it?" Denny moaned.

"Do what?" Julia asked.

"How does my dad keep messing up my life without even trying? He's been the bane of my existence ever since Mom left."

Julia looked surprised. "Your mom left?"

"Yeah. I was about nine when she took off."

"I'm so sorry," Julia sympathized.

Denny shook himself. "I don't want to talk about it." He took a deep breath, turned and smiled at her. "Let's find a way to get you back into the house before the Binders come home."

Julia looked at her wristwatch. "They said that the movie they were going to see was a two-hour one. If they come straight home, they should be here in the next…in the next fifteen minutes! Oh, Denny, what are we going to do?"

"Come on. Let's go see if there's a low window we can open."

The only possible one was a kitchen window, but without a stepladder, they couldn't reach it. Hand in hand, they wasted precious minutes looking up at the impossibly high window.

Julia cleared her throat. "Uh, maybe if I crawled onto your shoulders I could at least see if the window can be opened?"

Denny nodded and crouched down. Julia hesitated but a moment before she threw her legs around his neck.

"Ready?" he asked feeling a blush creep up his neck.

"I guess so."

"Quit wobbling!" Denny hissed.

"Well, I wouldn't wobble if you'd stand still!"

"I can't keep my balance when you're moving around! Ouch! Let go of my hair!"

"Denny, for God's sake, hold my legs! I'm slipping off!"

"Hold on!" Denny yelled.

Crashing to the ground, they landed in a heap on top of each other.

"You okay?" Denny asked.

Julia giggled. "Wow! That would have been fun to watch."

Denny looked at the laughing face so close to his, and he couldn't help himself. Days of thinking about her, nights of dreaming about her…he kissed her.

Surprised, Julia's body stiffened until she realized what had just happened. She looked into the soft brown eyes she had been fantasizing about, closed her own eyes, and murmured, "What took you so long?" And then she kissed him back.

More precious minutes passed. It was the sound of an automobile turning onto their street that ended their discovery of each other.

Denny's head went up. "They're here!"

"Oh, no!" Julia wailed. "Hey, wait a minute! I just remembered something!"

With that, she ran to the flower garden on the other side of the house, searched for a certain rock, found it, opened it up, and produced two keys. She handed one to Denny.

"There were keys there all along?" Denny looked puzzled.

"They've been there since I was in junior high but I never had to use them! I got locked out of my house one cold day after school, and the Binders weren't home. By the time Mom came home from work, I was pretty cold and scared. The keys have been inside that fake rock all these years!"

They could hear Judy and Joe chatting to each other about the movie as they unlocked the side door.

"Go, Julia, go!" urged Denny. He waited until the Binders were inside before he dashed across the distance to Susan's house.

Julia made it to the kitchen in time to grab a cup with the dregs of cold breakfast coffee in it. When Joe and Judy walked in, she was leaning her elbows on the kitchen counter struggling to hold the cup steady. Trying to keep the breathiness out of her voice, she asked, "How was the movie?"

"Great!" Joe answered. "Anything exciting happen while we were gone?"

Julia smiled with lips that were still tingling from Denny's kisses.

"Exciting? How could anything exciting happen when I can't leave the house?"

CHAPTER 41

Morning brought clear skies and a cold north wind. Ryan woke, shoved his head out of the warm sleeping bag, and pulled it back in.

Last night's supper of a lot of water and a little food was having an effect on his bladder. No matter how hard he tried to ignore the urge, he couldn't. With a groan, he crawled out into the cold air, looked with longing at the two sleeping bumps under his fur coat, and then headed into the woods to relieve himself.

Much later, Lynanne rolled over and bumped into Susan; Susan pushed her away. "Finally, you're awake!" she said to Lynanne. "I didn't want to wake you, but I really have to go!"

Lynanne stuck her head out of the coat. "Hey, it's not raining anymore," she exclaimed and then she ducked her head back under the coat.

"Come on, move! It's an emergency!" Susan poked her with her elbow.

"Ah, it's too cold out there!" Sensing that Susan was getting ready for another elbow punch, she huffed, "All right. I'm moving."

Feeling much relieved, Susan hurried back to find Lynanne sound asleep under the coat. Ryan's sleeping bag looked as if it were still zipped so he must be asleep, too.

Pulling close the warm jacket David had included in one of his garbage bag drops, she decided someone should be awake to keep her company. So, which one should she wake? Lynanne had been grumpy this morning, so she dismissed the idea of waking the still unmoving lump inside the coat. Did she have the nerve to wake Ryan? He certainly had made it clear that he didn't want to have anything to do with her. Oh, how she missed the old Ryan! He had said that he remembered everything. Everything? If he remembered everything, how could he act as if he hadn't said all those...those things, including the three little but very important words? And her face reddened when she remembered that she had repeated those same three words back to him. If he had chosen to forget, then she didn't have any reason to keep replaying those scenes over and over in her mind. But she wasn't sure how to forget about them.

She shook her head in resignation; she wasn't going to wake Ryan, either.

Instead, she lifted the edge of the coat, pushed Lynanne over, and crawled back into the warm nest.

* * * *

An hour later, Lynanne woke up, "Hey, sleepyhead," she shook Susan. "Wakey, wakey!"

"Wakey, wakey yourself!" Susan grumbled.

"Well, aren't we the cheerful one this morning!" Lynanne teased. "Hey, it looks like Ryan is still sleeping. I'm gonna wake him up, too!"

Susan had shut her eyes and was nodding off when Lynanne's cries startled her. "For heaven's sake, Lynanne...."

"He's gone! Ryan's gone!" Lynanne yelled.

Throwing the coat aside, Susan sat up. "He's probably just out in the woods relieving himself, so be quiet. You're scaring the birds."

Lynanne knelt down and felt the inside of the bag. "It's cold. Ryan's been gone for some time."

Susan got to her feet. "He can't be far. Let's just wait a bit before we get too excited."

* * * *

The sun was high in the sky before Susan would allow herself to believe that Ryan really wasn't coming back. Early in the search for him, they had found his jacket under a tree close to where they had spent the night.

"Why would he leave his jacket?" Lynanne kept asking.

A throbbing pain in Susan's heart made it hard for her to think. The night had been so cold, she knew that if Ryan had left the jacket on purpose, it was to tell them that something bad had happened to him…or maybe it got pulled off in a fight. She wouldn't let herself think about what was happening to Ryan right now if Ted had actually found him.

In the middle of the search, they had been aware of the activity at the landing strip. Planes had been coming and going since early morning.

"Do you think the DEA finally came?" Lynanne asked.

"Until your dad shows up, there's no way of knowing."

"If he's still alive," Lynanne's voice quivered. "What will we do if he never shows up?"

Susan put her arms around the girl. "Let's not go down that road until we absolutely have to."

"And what are we going to do about Ryan? I have a really bad feeling about him," Lynanne confessed.

"I do, too. Even though I know he dislikes me, I don't believe he would leave us both without saying something. At least I hope not."

"I didn't care for the way he was treating you," Lynanne continued. "I liked the old Ryan when he had amnesia. This new Ryan? Not so much."

It was late in the day before they gave up the search. They were sitting by the stream talking about imaginary food they wished they had when the sound of a tractor caught their attention.

"Dad?" Lynanne shouted.

The tractor, driven by someone they'd never seen before, broke through the underbrush and came to a halt beside them.

Lynanne's face turned white. "Something happened to Dad, didn't it?"

The driver crawled off the tractor, reached into his pocket, and produced his credentials. "I'm Special Agent Simon Hilburn with the Drug Enforcement Agency."

"Is Dad all right?" Lynanne asked anxiously.

"Miss, your dad is fine. He's working things out with the DEA and couldn't get away until they had them all settled. So he sent me."

Lynanne heaved a sigh of relief. "Thank God! Is the farm safe?"

"What was left of the workers has been rounded up, and the ones that were here to get the golfer are gone, too. By the way," he asked while looking around, "where is the third party? I was told I was to pick up three people."

Susan opened her mouth to tell the agent about Ryan, but her voice wouldn't work. Tears filled her eyes and ran down her cheeks. Putting into words the fact that Ryan was missing made it all too real. She couldn't pretend any more that he was going to walk through the trees and join them as if nothing had happened. Lynanne, seeing Susan's distress, stepped forward and explained to the agent that Ryan had been gone when they woke up this morning.

"Gone where?" Agent Hilburn's raised his eyebrows. "There's nowhere to go around here. I've never before been in such an isolated place in my life!"

"Tell me about it!" Lynanne rolled her eyes.

"Well, I'll take you two back to the farm and then I'll bring a search party back here."

Susan shrugged her shoulders and pointed. "We've searched all day and the only thing we found was his jacket over there."

The agent frowned. "It was cold this morning. Wonder why he left without his jacket? Are you thinking foul play?"

Susan nodded. "Ryan is the golfer the one group was looking for."

CHAPTER 42

Special Agent Simon Hilburn stopped the tractor by the front door of the farmhouse. "Miss, your dad is inside," he told Lynanne.

Susan was ready to walk into the house when she noticed that Lynanne wasn't beside her.

"Something wrong?" she asked the girl who was still standing by the tractor.

"Just remembering," Lynanne said softly. "You're standing in the same spot as Dad was that first day that we came here. That's when I saw the kitten and ran after it. When I looked back, three men had Dad and were tying him up." She shook her head. "So much has happened since then!"

"Then you've never been inside the house?" Susan asked.

"No, I haven't. Shall we?" She extended her arm to Susan.

When they walked through the door, David broke off speaking to a gentleman who seemed to be in charge. "Lynanne!" he cried.

Tears were streaming down both of their faces as they met in the middle of the kitchen and hugged. "It's all over, honey," he whispered in her ear. "We lived through it!"

The DEA agent watched the tearful reunion. "So, this is the girl you were bragging about?" he smiled and held his hand out. "I'm Agent Bell, by the way. And you! I'm proud to shake the hand of a girl who survived by living in a tree for over a year! Unbelievable!"

"Did I have a choice?"

"Probably not. You were safer in the tree than you would have been in this house. That was a nasty bunch of men who worked the fields," the agent said. "There wasn't one of them that I'd want to meet in a dark alley."

"Believe me, they were more vicious than nasty! I can show you graves. From high in my tree, I watched them bury people. I was always afraid they were going to look up and see the platform."

"We'll need to see those graves. With more things to charge them with, we can put these men in prison for the rest of their lives." Turning to Susan, he asked, "And who is this?"

Susan stepped forward. "I'm Susan Cook. I was with Ryan Wilcox when our plane crashed near the farm."

The agent's eyes widened. "Really? Ryan Wilcox, the golfer? He's been missing for about ten years."

"He wasn't missing; he was hiding. It's a long story, but he exposed a ring of sports gamblers who were injuring players to increase their chance of winning. Ryan was running from them when the plane crashed. I just happened to be with him when that happened."

"And where is Mr. Wilcox now? I'd love to meet him!"

Lynanne, seeing Susan tear up again, stepped in front of her and took over. "We're both pretty upset about Ryan right now, especially Susan. When we woke up this morning, Ryan was gone."

"Gone?" both David and the DEA agent spoke as one.

"No trace of him, except we found his jacket near our sleeping spot," Lynanne told them.

The agent raised his brows. "And you're thinking…what? Foul play?"

"One of the groups that came to the farm was here to capture or kill Ryan for money. There was a contract on Ryan's head."

The mention of a contract got the agent's attention. He pulled out his notebook and asked her for more details on the contract. Susan answered his questions as well as she could, but she knew that she lacked critical names and details. When it was clear that she had no more useful information to provide, he closed his notebook and gave Susan a moment to collect herself. Relating the circumstances behind Ryan's disappearance and possible death had left her struggling to control her emotions. No one said anything for a minute. Then the agent gently interrupted her thoughts. "Ms. Cook? You might as well fly out with us later today. Would that be all right with you?"

Susan didn't trust her voice. She just nodded. *Julia.* Her daughter's name was poised on her lips when she stopped herself. As far as Susan knew, her daughter was alive and well at home where she belonged. But what is she wasn't? Dare she ask the agent if he knew of any murders or bad things happening in the state of Michigan? *Be reasonable*, she thought. *Why would he know what was happening in Michigan? Quit thinking like a worried mother,* she told herself. If all went well, she and her daughter would soon be reunited.

"Do you have much luggage?"

Susan smiled sadly, as she held up the coat she had been carrying. "Just this."

The agent whistled. "That's quite a coat!"

"Would I have time to take a shower?" Susan asked. "We've been living quite rough for the past few days!"

"And we're hungry, too!" Lynanne piped up. "Any food, Dad?"

* * * *

Later that day, a much subdued Lynanne and Susan bid each other goodbye, each promising the other that they would stay in touch.

For the second time in her life, Susan boarded a small plane that, several hours later, deposited her at the airport of her hometown, a little jewel that nestled close to the big body of Lake Michigan.

The taxi taking Susan from the airport to her house slowed down when they entered her street. Susan's eyes reveled in the sight of her neighborhood. She hadn't been gone long, but so much had happened in those few days. A realtor's sign on one of the houses caught her attention. Why would the Watson's put their house on the market with another realtor? Jill was her friend! Her feelings were hurt.

Well, she thought, *You can't win them all, especially if you've been missing for a few days. Doesn't exactly inspire confidence.*

"It's the house with all the newspapers piled up by the front door," Susan told the driver. She could feel her nerves humming with anticipation; her daughter was behind that door. The cab pulled into her driveway and stopped. Her fare had been paid by the DEA agent, and with no luggage to retrieve, Susan, with the coat over her arm, climbed out of the backseat and waved at the driver as he backed out.

Susan stood outside her door and felt tears stinging her eyes. The last time she had run out this door she'd been with Ryan. Just thinking his name caused a pain in her heart.

The unlocked door swung open…and she found herself face to face with a complete stranger.

She screamed.

* * * *

Denny hadn't heard the cab pulling into Susan's driveway so when he heard the sound of the door being opened, his heart skipped a beat. Julia was paying him a visit!

Anticipating her greetings, he wasn't prepared mentally or physically for the sight or the sound of an unfamiliar screaming woman.

"Whoa!" Denny yelled as he backed up.

Susan stopped screaming. Whoever this kid was, he didn't look very threatening standing in her foyer in his bare feet.

"Whoa, yourself!" she exclaimed, clutching the coat as if it were a shield. "Who are you and what are you doing in my house?"

"Y...your house?" Denny took a closer look at the woman. Blonde hair, blue eyes… "Susan?" he asked tentatively.

She nodded.

His smile was radiant. "Susan! So you *are* alive!"

"Of course I'm alive!" Susan tried to look around Denny. "Is my daughter in there with you?"

"No she's not. She's next door."

"She's visiting Judy and Joe?"

"No, she's not visiting, she's hiding."

Susan's mouth dropped open.

Denny opened the door wider and motioned for Susan to enter the house.

"Mrs. Cook, I'd appreciate it if you'd come inside. I don't want to be seen."

He didn't want to be seen? Susan took two steps backwards and considered her odds. Even though the kid didn't look dangerous, for all she knew he could be Jack the Ripper. Whirling around, she sprinted toward the Binder house.

Denny's eyes followed the retreating Susan, heard her pound on the door, watched her being pulled inside by eager hands, and then listened to the squeals, shrieks and laughter that followed. The door shut, and Denny was all alone with more free time than he wanted. He cringed just thinking about how badly he had handled the situation. The only thing he had done well was scare Susan.

He hadn't minded the silence until now. Just imagining the joyous reunion going on next door made the quiet of Susan's house oppressive. Grabbing his shoes, he slipped them on his feet and ran to the Binder house.

CHAPTER 43

Dennis was grinning to himself as he approached his house. He'd done his job; the police were now looking for his son. All he had to do was to sit back and wait until they found him. And when they found Denny, he'd find Julia. He had to find her.

Of all the scams Dennis had going, the one with Julia could end it all. The girl had seen and experienced too much; she had to be taken out of the picture. And if that picture included his own son...well, so be it.

Seeing police cars parked in your own driveway wasn't something that most people would want to see, but to Dennis it meant one thing: they'd found Denny.

He pulled up to the curb in front of his house, got out of the car, and with a smile on his face, he extended his hand to a redheaded, green-eyed officer of the law. That officer accepted the offered hand, but instead of shaking it, he clasped a handcuff tightly around Dennis' wrist.

"Dennis McCain, you are under arrest."

Dennis sputtered. "For what? There's been a mistake!"

An older woman with a younger man beside her stepped up.

"There's no mistake!"

Oh, no! His eyes wild with panic, Dennis recognized the face but didn't remember the name of one of the widows he'd swindled. "What are you doing here?"

Mrs. Jack Freed shook her finger under his nose. "If you would have done some research, you would have found that my son is a CPA. It didn't take him long to figure out what you were doing!"

"But...but...I made lots of money for you!" Dennis tried to jerk away from the officer.

"You gave me other people's money!"

"I want my lawyer!" he was yelling as Officer Thomas Allen put a hand on Dennis' head and shoved him into the backseat of the squad car. "I *demand* my lawyer!"

With enough money, a good lawyer can sometimes make charges disappear. If that's not possible, a good lawyer can at least get you out on bail.

* * * *

Dennis was fuming in the backseat of the taxi. The stink of the holding cell had saturated his clothes and his soul; he could smell himself. How had he been found? Never had he worked under his own name. He didn't have an office, and all his stationery and his business cards had the address of a vacant lot on the other side of town. His cell phone? So much was going on in the electronics field it was hard to keep ahead of it. Had he been found through his phone?

He hadn't been paying attention to his trip home until a stop at a red light made him aware that they were in the vicinity of Susan's street; it was just a few blocks away. On an impulse, he instructed the cab driver to take a side trip. The cabbie shrugged. The meter was running so it was no concern of his.

In all of the times Dennis had checked Susan's house, he'd never seen any sign of activity. He wasn't really expecting to see anything today either, so when he saw a woman running from Susan's house heading for the idiots' house, he yelled, "Yes!"

"Yes?" repeated the cab driver. "You want me to stop?"

When the door on Susan's house opened and Denny ran out, Dennis laughed. "No, just get me home fast!"

He'd found his son and probably Julia. And if the woman was Susan, did that mean the golfer was there, too?

Could life get any sweeter? With the money he'd collect on the contract, he'd leave the country. If they wanted to put him in prison, they'd have to find him.

CHAPTER 44

Judy Binder was making the second pot of coffee, Joe was searching the pantry for another package of cookies, Denny was reveling in being so close to Julia, and mother and daughter were comparing war stories. Both Susan and Julia were leaving out parts of stories that not only would upset the listener, but would also distress the teller for having to relive the incident.

Susan's story of being chased by killers, surviving a plane crash, living in fear with a fifteen-year-old girl in a treehouse, and the Charles/Ryan amnesia situation vied with Julia's story of being kidnapped, how it felt to listen to men plotting your death, the kindness of the Binders, and being rescued by Denny not once but several times.

Susan glanced at Denny who was making love-eyes at her daughter. "I guess I should have been nicer to you when I opened the door," Susan chuckled. "So Denny, what's your full name?"

"My full name?" Denny's surprised look turned into a teasing one. "Why? Are you going to write me a big check?"

Susan laughed. "No, I'm not writing you a big check! But when a man looks at my daughter the way you do, I need to know his name."

Denny had the grace to blush. "My name is Dennis McCain."

Susan's reaction to the name was instant. "Oh my God!" With that, she clutched her daughter. "Dennis McCain...that's the name of the man that I was told killed you! What is he doing living in my house?"

"Mother, settle down! Dennis McCain Junior is living in your house. Dennis McCain Senior is Denny's father."

"Oh." Susan sat for a bit, looking at Denny. "I guess I didn't make the connection when you were telling me how Denny had saved you from being killed. Are you saying Denny rescued you from his own father?"

"Yes, Mom, Denny's father is evil. I do believe he'd have no second thoughts about killing his own son."

Denny had listened to the conversation without saying a word. Embarrassing as it was, hearing someone else accusing his father of being a ruthless killer, even though it was true, still didn't sit well.

Susan asked, "And why were you kidnapped in the first place?"

Leaning forward, Julia asked earnestly, "You do know that there's a contract on your golfer friend, don't you?"

Hearing her daughter calling Ryan "your golfer friend" brought back vivid memories; the pain was so sharp she groaned.

"Mother, what's wrong with you?" Julia yelled.

With her eyes shut, Susan was remembering Ryan's laughing face, his tender lovemaking under the coat, and her body's reaction to the words he'd whispered in her ear. He had made her feel alive. It was as if she had been emotionally asleep for years, and with one kiss, Ryan had awakened her.

With a great effort, Susan regained her composure. "It's all right, honey. Must have been something I ate. Yes, I know about the contract. What does that have to do with you?"

"One of the brighter ones came up with the idea that since I'm your daughter, I might know where you and your golfer friend went."

"Ah, yes. I do remember Charles telling me that you might be in danger. But you didn't know where we were."

"Well, they figured that out, but I had seen too many of them, and a lot of them are local people. I do believe a few of the town's police force are on their payroll."

"That's not good, honey! Are you still in danger?"

"Very much so. Denny's dad keeps driving up and down the street. He figures I'm around here someplace."

"Why hasn't he checked my house? That would be the most logical place where you would go."

"He has, Mother. He has checked both your house and the Binder house."

"And?"

"And what?"

"Why didn't he find you?"

"Denny managed it, Mom."

"My, my!" Susan looked at Denny. "With every story, I'm getting more impressed with you."

Julia blushed.

Susan smiled. "So it's like that, is it?"

"You don't mind?" Julia asked shyly.

Susan shook her head. Before Ryan and also because mothers do things like that, she probably would have lectured Julia and Denny about age, maturity, and responsibility, but not now. Who was she to deny anyone those wonderful feelings?

Susan looked at her watch. "I need to run back home and take a shower."

Julia examined her mother. "In all the excitement, I just now noticed that you're wearing an over-sized sweatsuit that I've never seen before."

Susan looked down at her legs and remembered Ryan's laughing face looking up at her as he rolled-up her too long pants. "It's more fun taking these off you than putting them back on," he had said to her.

"Mother, why in the world are you blushing?"

"Oh, I…, nothing, honey. There's a story about a skunk in my flower bed…but I'll tell you about it later."

"A skunk?" Julia looked puzzled.

Before Susan could reply, Denny interrupted. "I'm going with you," Seeing the look on Susan's face, he added, "With your permission, of course."

Susan grinned. "I'd be honored to hide my daughter's knight-in-shining-armor."

Julia already knew the answer to her next question because she'd been in Susan's house. "How are you fixed for groceries?"

Susan stopped, hit her head with her hand. "I just remembered that my purse burned up in the crash. I have no driver's license, no identification, no cash, no credit cards, no car...."

"No car?" questioned Julia. "That's right, a taxi brought you home. What happened to your car?"

Susan waved her hand to dismiss the question. "Honey, we don't have enough time to get into that. How I lost my car is part of a much bigger story. Just know that I have to get a new one."

Judy stepped in. "Make a list, and I'll go to the store for you. Tomorrow is soon enough for you to worry about your missing things."

Susan grabbed Judy and hugged her. "Oh, thank you, Judy! How will I ever repay you for keeping my daughter safe?"

"It's not all over yet, so why don't you wait to thank me when it is?"

Susan gave Julia one last hug. Denny wanted to do the same thing, but with Susan's eyes on him, he didn't have the nerve.

The two of them walked back to Susan's house.

CHAPTER 45

Dennis jumped out of the taxi and rushed into his house. He needed to get back before the reunion ended at the idiots' house. Should he call others for backup? No. If he included others, then he'd have to share the contract money, and if he intended to disappear when it was all over, he'd need every penny of it. But what if the golfer wasn't with Susan? There was no price on Julia's head, she just needed to be silenced. Did that mean that, without payment, he'd still have to do away with Julia, and probably Denny?

Pulling into Susan's street, he slowed down. He needed to find a parking spot less than a block from Susan's house. If he had to make a speedy departure, he didn't want to have to run a footrace to his car.

As he approached her house, he walked casually, trying to look as if he belonged in the neighborhood. And if someone did see him, he didn't want to look interesting enough for the person to remember anything about him.

He arrived at Susan's door with the credit card already in his hand. The door opened on the first try. Man, he was getting good at this!

After a quick tour assured him that the house was empty, he pulled out a chair at the kitchen table and sat down. Now he would wait until someone walked through the door. If they entered singly, he could handle them one at a time. He arranged his arsenal on the table, sat back in his chair and waited.

Dennis, having spent a sleepless night in the jail's holding tank waiting to be bailed out, was sleepier than he realized. It was just a matter of time before his head went down on the table.

Once again, Dennis slept.

* * * *

Susan and Denny walked back to her house in silence. Susan knew the door wasn't locked, so without a word being said, she opened it and motioned for Denny to go in first. It was her way of telling him that she had accepted the fact that he'd be living with her.

Denny stopped so suddenly, Susan ran into him.

"Move it!" she muttered.

Instead, Denny backed up. Scrambling to get out of his way, she was about to voice her objection when his hand slapped down on her mouth. Thoughts of Jack the Ripper flashed once again through her head as he proceeded to back out, pulling the door after him.

"What th…!" she yelled after he removed his hand.

"Shhhh! My dad is in your house!"

"No!"

"Yes he is! He's sound asleep, and after seeing what's on the table in front of him, I suggest we get help before he wakes up."

"Oh my God! What should we do?"

Denny thought hard. Who on the police force was clean? He had no idea.

"Susan, do you personally know anyone at the police station who might not be involved in this mess?"

Susan was breathing hard. When was her life going to get boring again? When it did, she resolved that never again would she complain about it.

"I don't know! Wait a minute. Julia told me about a young policeman who came to the school to talk about bike safety. The kids loved him. She mentioned that he had red hair and green eyes. But that's a description, not a name."

"I'll stay here. You run next door and call for help. Maybe Julia will remember the cop's name, but if not, how many redheaded-green-eyed cops would they have in a town this size?"

"Are you sure you'll be all right by yourself?"

Denny shrugged. "I'll be okay. After all, it is my dad we're talking about."

Denny watched Susan as she ran through the yard and over the driveway and then into the house. He was content to wait patiently for a while, but then the desire to go into the house and watch his dad sleep came over him. That was his dad in there with his head on the table. His dad. He hadn't been the best dad in the world, but he'd kept him clothed and fed. True, there was no love, but wasn't sharing the same blood supposed to be thick enough to hold families together? Then again, his mother had left him.

Expecting to see his dad still asleep at the table when he reentered the house, he was momentarily stunned when he realized that no one was sitting there.

"Dad? Dad?" he called softly.

"I'm here, son," said a voice that sounded so much like Denny's own voice it was eerie. Before he could turn around, a blow to his head knocked him senseless.

* * * *

"No, no, Susan! Don't go back to your house! Wait for the cops to get here!" pleaded Joe Binder.

"But it's my house, and I left Denny over there all alone."

"Mom, please listen to Joe!" Julia cried. "Dennis McCain Sr. is pure evil! Believe me. The men who were holding me captive were scared to death of him."

"Well, I'll just run over and make sure Denny's all right. We'll wait outside until the police get here." With that, Susan ran out of the house and didn't slow down until she reached her own door.

Surprise was her first reaction when Denny was nowhere to be seen; fear was her second. Denny wouldn't go into the house, would he? Did he believe that because it was his own dad nothing bad would happen to him?

Waking Dennis was the last thing she wanted to do. Opening the door as quietly as she could, she took a tentative step inside.

"Welcome!" cackled Dennis. The bat that landed on Susan's head was one that he'd found in Julia's closet. She had used a black magic marker to print her name on the handle. To use her own daughter's bat to render her unconscious was, in his opinion, pure brilliance.

Dennis was pleased. This was working out better than he thought it would. After he duct taped Susan's hands, he propped her up against the wall and applied a cold cloth to her forehead. Since she was the one who would know where the golfer and Julia were hiding, he hadn't hit her nearly as hard as he'd hit Denny. The kid hadn't moved.

Susan's eyes popped open. How had she gotten here on the floor? And why did her head hurt?

In a friendly voice, Dennis greeted her, "Hello, Susan. Welcome to my world."

Looking up, Susan saw a blurred figure standing over her. It took several seconds for her eyes to focus. "Denny?"

"No, not Denny. I'm Dennis, his dad."

"B...but you look just like him!"

"So we've been told. Susan, do you feel up to answering a few questions?"

Susan raised her taped hands. "Do I have a choice?"

"Not really."

"So? Ask me."

"I have questions about your golfing friend."

Tears filled Susan's eyes and ran down her cheek. "What do you want to know about my golfing friend?"

"Where is he?"

Susan burst into tears.

"Come, now. Why the tears? It can't be that bad!"

"Why do you want to know where he is?"

"Why do I want to know? Susan, Susan. Surely you know there's a big price on his head! Someone's going to collect it, and I've decided that it's going to be me."

Susan's switched from crying to laughing, and then back to crying.

A slap on her face startled her. Trying to wipe her eyes with her sleeve, she stopped and looked up at him. "Why did you do that?"

"Cut out the hysterics! Where is your golfing friend?"

"He's nowhere as far as you're concerned. Someone beat you to him."

"What?" screamed Dennis. "We would have been told if someone had him!"

"You're sure about that? All I know is that he disappeared. One morning, he was just gone."

"You're lying!" he screamed and hit her again.

"I'm not lying! He's gone!" Susan groaned.

Poised to strike again, Dennis' hand stopped in mid air. What was that noise? Running to the window, he looked out to see a squad car coming to an abrupt stop by the Binder house.

Who had called the police? Who even knew he was here? This wasn't supposed to happen. He couldn't be caught here! Weren't there laws about people who were out on bail? Being caught with a gun and unconscious victims would throw him right back in jail. The back door! He'd slip out the back door. Maybe they wouldn't see him running to his car.

He turned to leave, only to stumble over his own son who was pointing a gun at him. His own son, and his own gun. No! Wait a minute. Denny's hands were shaking. Would his dumbass kid have the nerve to shoot him?

Full of confidence, Dennis laughed at Denny as he ran for the back door. Turning his head to look back over his shoulder, he sneered, "Forget about it, son. You don't have the guts to shoot your own dad!"

No one was more surprised than Denny when he pulled the trigger.

CHAPTER 46

Denny, who had never before held a gun let alone fired one, was more than surprised when the gun's recoil threw him backward onto the floor. Dazed, he lay for a moment in complete shock until the sound of someone screaming cut into his stupor.

The first thing he saw when he sat up was the hand that his dad was holding to his own face had blood spurting out through its fingers. The second thing he saw was a redheaded policeman rushing across the room and arresting his dad. Still suffering from the blow to his head and horrified by knowledge that he'd shot his own dad, he sought refuge in nothingness and loss consciousness.

****

Susan stood with her arms around Julia and watched the two ambulances pull away with Dennis and a police escort in one, and Denny in the other. At first, Denny had protested, insisting that there was nothing wrong with him, but when the attendant checked his eyes and saw unequal pupils, Denny no longer had any say in the decision. Julia had wanted to go with him. "You can't expose yourself, love," he reminded her. "You still are the only one who can identify the locals who are involved in the mess."

Officer Tom Allen and Detective Mitch Hatch joined Julia and Susan. "With all this going on, why didn't someone call for police protection?"

Julia stopped walking. "You really don't know?" she asked.

Detective Hatch raised his eyebrows. "Know what?"

Susan and Julia exchanged glances. Detective Hatch and Officer Allen needed to be told about the local people, including cops, who were involved.

Susan cleared her throat. "Gentlemen, if you'll follow me to my kitchen I will brew us a pot of coffee; Julia and I have stories to tell you."

* * * *

Mother and daughter watched the police officer and the detective walk to their cars.

"Do you think they believed us?" Julia wondered.

Susan took a deep breath. "You have Denny to back up your story. I have no one."

"Mom?"

"Yes?"

"You loved him, didn't you?"

Tears were streaming down Susan's cheek.

"Very much."

"What do you really think happened to him?"

Susan wiped her eyes. "T…Ted is what happened to him."

Julia allowed Susan to regain her composure before she said, "Mom, have you charged your phone since you've been home?"

Susan raised her eyebrows. "Well, yes I have. That's a strange question."

"Not so strange, Mom. In your story, you tell how Ryan made a call to the only number he could remember. It was to his old home where Ted and Laura now live."

Susan nodded. "So?"

"So? You have that number on your phone."

The light went on in Susan's eyes. "To do what with it?"

"I don't know…but if you think Ted really did something to Ryan, you could share that number with the detective."

"Without a body to prove anything, what good would come of it?"

"Maybe scare him? That would be better than doing nothing!"

Susan reached for her cell phone. "Grab a piece of paper and a pen. Let's write the number down, and when you go to the station tomorrow to look at pictures, you can give it to Officer Tom."

* * * *

Between obsessing over the fact that he'd shot his own father and the night nurse waking him to shine a light into his eyes every time he dropped off to sleep, his one night in the hospital was a complete bust; he couldn't wait to be discharged. He left the hospital at noon with a firm belief that only a healthy person could survive a longer stay.

Before he left, he inquired about Dennis Sr.

The nurse at the desk picked up a clipboard and then looked up at him. "Uh, that particular patient is in police custody on the sixth floor."

"Does it say on the chart what condition he's in?"

Looking over her glasses, the nurse informed him that only close relatives were permitted to have such information.

It took courage for Denny to say, "I'm his son."

The nurse gave him a pitying look.

"Write your name on the visitor's chart. His room number is 615."

Denny hesitated. Did he really want to see the man he'd shot? He had visions of Dennis jumping out of bed and choking him to death.

He straightened his shoulders and headed for the elevator. Getting off on the sixth floor, he saw that room 615 was right across the hall. The uniformed policeman who sat outside the room looked up from what he was reading. With a startled cry, he jumped up, looked inside the room to make sure the prisoner was still chained to the bed and then back at Denny.

Flopping down on his chair, he wiped his brow. "Son, you gave me the scare of my life!"

Denny stood in the open doorway and studied the man shackled to the bed. He knew it, but his dad had no idea that Detective Hatch was busy digging into his past history. Already he'd come up with a witness who could identify Dennis as the one who had taken the first and last month's rent on a house he didn't own. If the detective found one victim, he was sure he could find others. They already had Mrs. Jack Freed, the widow who'd been fleeced out of her money in the investment pyramid scheme. Add all of that to what he did to Julia, and Denny knew his dad would be behind bars for years.

Pointing to the side of his dad's bandaged face, he asked the guard, "What does the doctor say about his face?"

"Well, his ear, his cheek, and one side of his nose are gone. One thing for sure, he'll never look the same again."

"Good!" exclaimed Denny.

He crossed the hall and stepped into the waiting elevator.

CHAPTER 47

The broker at Susan's real estate office welcomed her back with a hug and a potted plant for her desk.

"We missed you, Susan! Welcome back."

Susan made room for the plant on her desk. "Thank you, Martha. I'm glad to be back."

"That was quite an adventure you had!"

"An adventure?" Susan raised her eyebrows. "Well, I guess you could call it that."

Martha's mouth was moving, but Susan wasn't listening. A series of pictures were flashing through her mind. There was Ryan smiling down at her, Ryan pulling her back under the coat, Ryan kissing her, Ryan....

"....and so that's what happened while you were gone. But your partner Zena took care of it for you. If you'd share part of the commission with her, she'd appreciate it. Well, I'll leave you now. You have a lot of catching up to do."

Susan sat down at her desk and stared off into space. The frustration of not being able to search for him was eating at her very soul. She'd lost the great love that had put meaning in her life; now her world was colorless. Without Ryan, did she even want to live?

But wait a minute. Was Ryan *really* dead? What if the contract people hadn't grabbed him but his old golfing buddies had? They could have done that, couldn't they? Maybe they were hiding Ryan from the contract people. They could be doing that, couldn't they? If that was so, then Ryan was alive, and it was just a matter of time before he came back to her. That's what was happening, wasn't it?

The sense of urgency that hit her was as strong and painful as a physical blow. What was she doing here? Ryan might be on his way to her right now.

Susan got up from her desk, grabbed her purse and her coat, and rushed out of the office.

* * * *

Julia left the police station feeling safer than she'd felt in a long time. Her mind was numb from looking at hundreds of pictures; it had been time well spent. With the exception of Old Blue Eyes, she'd been able to pick out the faces of the locals who'd been involved in her kidnapping. The response to her description of him produced only blank faces. They had no knowledge of the person with eyes like Alaskan sled dogs. What they did learn from interrogating those who had been lured by the promise of easy money was that the hunt for the golfer had been called off.

Feeling like a ton of weight had been lifted from her shoulders, she dropped into the real estate office to share the good news with her mother.

She waved her way past Emma at the front desk on her way to her mom's office in the back. With a smile on her face, she peered through the open door and stopped. Susan wasn't there. Stepping back in surprise, she bumped into someone.

"Oh, Emma, excuse me! I didn't know you were behind me!"

"Don't worry, no harm done," Emma grinned. "Looking for your mom?"

"Yes, I am. But I'm surprised that Mom isn't at her desk. I know she was fussing about all the work that had piled up while she was gone."

"That's why I followed you back here. Do you have any idea why she rushed off? She tore out of here as if someone were chasing her!"

Julia shook her head. "Maybe she came back to work too soon. I've been so worried about her, I've moved back home."

Emma's face clouded. "I'm sorry to hear that, Julia. I know how much you were enjoying being on your own."

Julia tried to keep the disappointment out of her voice. "Well, it's not as if I can't move out again."

Emma nodded and patted Julia's shoulder.

Julia regained her composure. "What she went through in the past few days was pretty horrific."

"I understand you had a pretty rough time yourself, hon," Emma added quietly.

Julia nodded while she thought about the one big difference in their misadventures; her own heart had found love while her mother's heart had been broken.

"If she needs a few days off, is there someone here who can do her work?"

"Zena is her partner. I'm sure she won't mind continuing to do that for Susan."

"I'd better go home and see if that was where she went."

"Will you keep us informed?"

"I'm sure in a few days Mom can do that herself."

****

Julia rushed home to an empty house. That was strange, because Susan's car was parked in the garage. With just one more place to look, Julia was getting worried. This was so unlike her mother.

The place she had yet to search was the front porch. The weather had turned quite cold and Julia felt silly checking it. There would be no reason for Susan to be sitting on the swing this time of year.

But she was. Huddled in Ryan's fur coat, she was staring straight ahead.

"Mom," Julia called, "What are you doing out here? Come into the house where it's warm. Anyhow, I have stuff to tell you and I have no intention of freezing my butt off."

"That's nice, honey," Susan replied.

"That's nice? What kind of an answer is that?"

"That's nice, honey," Susan repeated.

"Mom!" Julia shook her. "Mom! What's wrong?"

Susan looked up. "Oh, hi! Did you just get home?"

"Yes. What are you doing out here?"

"Nothing that concerns you," Susan assured her in a flat voice. "Go back inside. I'll be with you in a minute."

And in a minute, Susan did go back inside. What she did then was to retire to her room, and without undressing, she wrapped the coat around her and crawled into bed.

Before Julia went to work the next morning, she checked on her mother. Susan was still asleep, wrapped in the coat.

* * * *

Julia came home from school a few weeks later to find Susan with her head on her desk and the phone in her hand.

"Hey, Mom!" Julia called. "You're home early. What happened…your buyers cancel on you?"

"What? Oh, hi, honey. I didn't hear you come in."

"I guess what I'm asking is what are you doing home so early?"

"I…I never went to work today."

Julia stepped closer and looked at her mother. "Are you not feeling well?"

Susan shrugged. "There's nothing wrong. Going to work just doesn't seem that important anymore."

"Mom, I know you're having a…"

"That will be enough out of you, young lady! None of this 'I know' business!"

Julia opened her mouth.

"I said enough!"

"Okay, Mom. Uh, can we talk about why you have the phone in your hand?"

Susan looked puzzled. "I guess I forgot to hang it up. Sorry."

"And you couldn't hear the beeping noise coming out of the phone?"

"I wasn't paying attention. I was thinking about the call I'd just had."

"Wanna tell me about it?"

"Remember we gave Officer Tom the number I had on my phone?"

"I do. It was Ted and Laura's number. Did the cop find anything?"

"Other than a vacant house, nothing. It looks like Ted and Laura split. No one has any idea where they went."

"Do you think that means they cashed in on the contract?"

"No, I don't. Because that would mean that Ryan is dead, and I know he's not."

"You know he's not? Mom, you may not want to think of him as dead, but what proof do you have?"

Tapping her finger on the side of her head, she whispered, "Because I just know!"

"No, Mom, you don't just know! You're scaring me."

"If Ryan were dead, I'd know."

Julia rolled her eyes. "I'm going to the kitchen to start dinner. Any suggestions?"

"I'm not really hungry, so don't cook for me. If you want me, I'll be out on the swing."

"It's freezing outside!"

"I have my coat."

Julia said softly, "I know you're waiting for him."

"Julia, enough!"

As time went on, Susan's actions didn't change. It worried Julia to leave for work in the morning while her mother was still in bed. She found her many times at the computer, checking areas close and sometimes not so close for any activity that included the names Ted and Laura. Susan was well aware that without Ted's last name, she was at a disadvantage, but there was a fifty-fifty chance that it would be Wilcox, just like Ryan's. And then there was the fact that the name Ted was just a nickname for Theodore. Although Susan spent hours searching, the two names never appeared in a news story.

Sometimes Susan did drag her body out of bed and go to work, but her heart wasn't in it. She was no longer the top producing agent in her office, the position she had held with so much pride. The only reason her name was on the list at all was because a returning customer or a referral from a former customer had especially asked for her.

Julia watched her mother gradually removing herself from social activities. At first, concerned friends and co-workers called, but when Susan showed no interest in staying in contact with them, the calls stopped.

Julia, as a child, had a comfort blanket. Susan, as an adult, had a comfort coat. Just as Julia had clutched her blanket, Susan now hugged her coat. They were living on the commission of the few houses that Susan sold and Julia's paycheck. Julia had given up trying to talk to her mother about her behavior; all suggestions about seeking professional help fell on deaf ears.

CHAPTER 48

Susan found refuge in sleep. Julia watched her vibrant and active mother retreating from the world. When Susan's face became animated while she slept, Julia wondered about her mother's dreams. Wonder was all she could do; Susan refused to talk about them.

Sleep came quickly to Susan, and with sleep came dreams of Ryan. In those dreams, the dreadful morning when he had gone missing had been deleted. Instead, he had been inside the sleeping bag when Lynanne had gone to wake him. The Ryan who woke was the old Ryan who loved her. In her dreams, all was wonderful…especially what went on when they cuddled together under the coat.

Waking up to a life without Ryan was cruelly harsh. All she could think about was returning to Ryan in her dream world. Her most vivid dreams came to her while she was wrapped in the coat, sitting on the porch swing. In those dreams, Ryan was real.

* * * *

One morning, Susan woke with a start. She could hear Julia, her voice loud in protest, talking on the telephone. A glance at the clock told Susan if she were going to work today, and that was iffy, she'd better get up. The work debate that was going on in her head came to a halt when she heard Julia cry, "Denny, please tell me you didn't mean that! Hello? Hello? Denny, did you hang up on me?"

Julia's tears registered in Susan's motherly soul. Dragging herself out of bed, she chanced to look into the mirror on her dresser. Looking back at her was a disheveled and sad looking woman who, she knew, hadn't brushed her teeth or taken a shower in days. It was then that she was hit with the strong and very real feeling that Ryan wasn't pleased with how she was handling his absence. The message was so clear, she didn't even think it strange that he had voiced an opinion. And then there was Julia; she deserved something better. If she was upset enough to cry, she needed a strong mother and that's not what Susan saw staring back at her.

Later, over coffee and toast, Julia wiped the last tears from her eyes and looked across the table, expecting to see her mother in her ratty housecoat. Instead, sitting there was a very attractive woman with shiny clean hair and a face that glowed with subtle makeup, lipstick, and mascara.

"Mom?" Julia sniffed.

"I heard you crying, Julia. I don't know what it was about, but it got to me."

"Mom, I know your heart is broken. I just wish I could have met your love. He must have been something very special."

"Yes, he is."

Julia chose to ignore that her mother had spoken of Ryan in the present tense. "I suppose you heard my phone call this morning?"

"Yes, and I heard you crying."

"Mom, it was our very first fight, and the dispute we were having was about you!"

"Me?"

"Denny had a therapist lined up to pay you a visit."

"He didn't!"

"He did. I told him you shouldn't be confronted with a therapist without being told beforehand, and he was insisting that was the only way to get to you."

"Oh, my. I'm that bad?"

"You have us all worried."

"I'm going to be all right, Julia. Would you please tell Denny thanks but no thanks for the therapist?"

"Are you sure?"

Susan smiled." I'm sure."

"Are you going in to work today?" Julia asked as she picked up her car keys.

"You know what? I think I'm going to take a few weeks off. Zena can take care of my work a bit longer. After all, I did her work for most of the nine months she carried her last child."

"Are you not feeling well, Mom?" Julia had an anxious look on her face.

"I'm fine, honey. I think a few weeks off work is what I need right now."

"Are you sure that's all it is?"

"Quit worrying about me! I'm fine!"

She smiled a sweet smile as her daughter walked out the door, on her way to her raucous eighth graders.

Susan knew enough to keep her mouth shut. How her heart knew, she didn't question.

Ryan wasn't dead.

CHAPTER 49

The warm days of spring melted the last piles of dirty white snow in Susan's neighborhood. Soon the trees would be budding, the birds would be building nests, and the brutal winter would be talked about in the past tense.

Free from even thinking about going to work, Susan spent most of her days sitting on the porch swing bundled up in the coat. Professional jealousy had reared its ugly head the morning the realtor arrived at the house across the street and slapped a sold sticker on the sign. It still didn't sit well with her that her neighbor had chosen to list their house with another realtor.

A few days later, carpenters arrived and built a ramp up to the porch. Directly after that, a van pulling into her new neighbor's driveway caught her attention. A man in a white coat went around to the back, opened the door, pulled down a ramp, and unloaded a wheelchair; the man who occupied the chair was strapped in. She could see that there was a black patch over one of the man's eyes, and his hanging head bobbed as the chair bumped over the cracks in the sidewalk. The attendant stooped to wipe drool off the man's chin before he pushed the wheelchair up the ramp and into the house.

Curious about her new neighbor, Susan spent even more time on the swing. Huddled inside the warm coat, she watched and waited patiently, hoping the attendant would push the wheelchair onto the front porch. After a few days, a schedule seem to be established; if the man appeared at all, it was mid-morning.

It became a ritual. Susan made sure she was already on the swing before the man appeared. Every morning she waved at him, and because he never waved back, she wondered if he could even see her. On the days that he didn't appear, she was surprised how much it bothered her. She had no idea why she felt so content when he was there, and why the sense of urgency was so great when he wasn't.

She often fantasized about walking across the street and visiting him. Maybe she could take a casserole with her as an excuse for the visit. She thought about it so much that one morning she found the courage to leave her swing. Clutching the coat in her arms, she made it to the middle of the street where she stopped, and then for some reason she didn't understand, she turned and fled back to her swing.

One morning the man in the wheelchair who'd survived a beating that was meant to kill him looked across the street with his one good eye, and was disturbed when he saw that the swing was empty.

His mind went back to the time when it looked as if she were coming to see him; his heart had almost stopped beating. Dare he believe that she could feel his presence? What had made her turn back? Eventually he wanted her to see him, but not like this.

Anxiety over the empty swing disappeared when the door opened and Susan, with a cup of coffee in her hand, stepped out. For a while he had been troubled about her disheveled appearance. Today, she was fine; she was once again his beautiful Susan. He followed her eyes as they searched for him, and when they found him, he tried to nod his head. The love he felt for her was the strongest part of his wrecked body. The one muscle that was still working was his tongue; he slipped it out and caught the salty tear that was running down his cheek.

It pleased him that even though it was a warm morning, she was still wearing his coat.

A Message From The Author:

ACKNOWLEDGEMENTS

Writing is a lonely but almost God-like occupation. To inhabit the writer's imaginary world, living, breathing characters who have names, attribute, and personalities are created. And then, like God, the writer has the power to choose which of them will succeed, which ones will fail, which ones will find love, which ones will have their heart's broken, and which ones won't make it to the end of the story.

Writing might be a lonely occupation, but it's an exciting one.

The writing bug didn't bite me until I was well into retirement. But once it bit, it became an obsession. A day without writing, to me, is a day without sunshine. I had never written a short story, but once I started, I couldn't stop. My first venture was writing the six books in The Accidental Mystery Series.

I have a circle of friends that not only are very supportive, they also keep my feet planted firmly on the ground. They are not afraid to tell me when I go off the deep end with a plot or a character, and they have very sharp red correcting pencils. When I told them that I had written another book, maybe the start of a new series, a few of them rolled their eyes. I think I've worn them out.

While writing The Coat, I sent sections as I wrote them to Judy Freed and Pat Bell for corrections and feed back. One of the first drafts was read by Pat Batta who writes The Marge Christensen Mystery Series, Jody Clark who was the leader of my writing group, my daughter Jill who is a much better writer than her mother, my husband Barry who has a keen eye for errors, and Karen Fritz. Karen is also my word person; she never lets me down.

When my manuscript was accepted for publication by Ink-Smith Publishing, the person I was assigned to work with was Corinne Anderson. Corinne breathed fresh air into my plot, she rearranged chapters, and helped me add color to the characters. The Coat is a much better book because of her.

Rowenna Dodge Anderson, a nationally known artist, has been a dear friend of mine since college days. She was my roommate and also part of my college traveling trio. When I told her I was having problems coming up with a cover for The Coat, she volunteered to create one for the price of a free book. You can see her art at http://www.jtodd.com/products.asp?cat=146&hierarchy=&p=2. Her works are in many private collections throughout the United States and Europe.

They say write about what you know. I sold real estate for fifteen years in Rochester, Michigan. The action in The Accidental Mystery Series originated out of Allen Real Estate. Susan, the main character in The Coat, is also a realtor but works at a different office in the same western Michigan town. The connection between the first series and The Coat is very subtle. If you hadn't read the series, then when Susan picks up a key to show one of Allen's listings and finds a huge dog named Lucky asleep in the corner, it would mean nothing to you. But to readers of the series, it would be like visiting a much-loved old friend.

Do you have any idea how much authors appreciate feedback from readers? After you've read The Coat, write to me at evharp@hotmail.com. I value your comments and I promise to write back.

www.ingramcontent.com/pod-product-compliance
Lightning Source LLC
Chambersburg PA
CBHW031222260626
47169CB00007B/2151